Shear Bliss
Foggy Basin Series
Sam E. Kraemer

Kaye Club Publishing

Copyright

This book is an original work of fiction. Names, characters, places, incidents, and events are the product of the author's imagination and are used fictitiously. Any resemblance to actual persons, living or dead, business establishments, events, or locales is entirely coincidental.

Copyright ©2024 by Sam E. Kraemer

Cover Designer: Covers by Jo, Jo Clement

Formatter: TL Travis

Editor: Abbie Nicole, ASP

Proofreaders: Mildred Jordan, I Love Books Proofreading

Published by Kaye Klub Publishing

All products/brand names mentioned in this work of fiction are registered trademarks owned by their respective holders/corporations/owners. No trademark infringement intended.

No part of this book may be reproduced, scanned, or distributed in any form, printed or electronic, without the express permission of the publisher. Please do not participate in or encourage piracy of copyrighted materials in violation of the author's rights. Purchase only authorized editions.

Note: NO AI/NO BOT. The author does not consent to any Artificial Intelligence (AI), generative AI, large language model, machine learning, chatbot, or other automated analysis, generative process, or replication program to reproduce, mimic, remix, summarize, or otherwise replicate any part of this creative work, via any means: print, graphic, sculpture, multimedia, audio, or other medium without express permission from the author. I support the right of humans to control their artistic works.

Blurb

Ex-con turned barber Tyler Rockwell works in his mother's beauty salon in small-town California. Every resident of Foggy Basin will happily remind Tyler they know the one thing he wants to put behind him.

Mosby Leslie left his old life behind after a tragedy, hiding in the mountains near Foggy Basin, where the fog rolled into the valley like clockwork. Committed to living alone in misery, Mosby fills his days with painting landscapes of the sleepy little village he can see from his front porch and having intense discussions with Barbara Bushy, his only friend.

One day while on a supply run, Mosby trips over a crumbling step in front of Shear Bliss Salon, hitting his head. Next thing he knows, a handsome young man is tending to his every need. The shorter, lean man's smiles light up Mosby's sullen world.

To stay in the sunshine of Tyler's attention for just a little longer, Mosby pretends to have forgotten who he is and where he lives. What will the barber do when he finds out that under Mosby's long hair and beard is a famous painter who people have been trying to find for over a year? When the fog clears, is there any way the two of them can find Shear Bliss together?

Welcome to Foggy Basin. Just passing through? No problem. Here to stay? Well, better find your place. Sit back, relax, and get to know the townsfolk. They love hard and play even harder. Each book is a stand-alone but why not stay and get to know us by reading them all.

POSSIBLE TRIGGERS: This story contains scenes depicting sexual harassment in the workplace, and discussions of violence and abuse while incarcerated. Reader discretion is advised.

Contents

1. Prologue — 1
2. Chapter One — 5
3. Chapter Two — 18
4. Chapter Three — 29
5. Chapter Four — 40
6. Chapter Five — 50
7. Chapter Six — 61
8. Chapter Seven — 78
9. Chapter Eight — 91
10. Chapter Nine — 102
11. Chapter Ten — 112
12. Chapter Eleven — 124
13. Chapter Twelve — 145
14. Chapter Thirteen — 162
15. Chapter Fourteen — 173

16.	Chapter Fifteen	182
17.	Chapter Sixteen	194
18.	Chapter Seventeen	204
19.	Chapter Eighteen	214
20.	Chapter Nineteen	226
21.	Chapter Twenty	237
22.	Chapter Twenty-One	246
23.	Chapter Twenty-Two	248
24.	Epilogue	254
About Sam E. Kraemer		260
Also by Sam E. Kraemer/L.A. Kaye		261

Prologue

Mosby Leslie

February 2023

A ringing phone at four in the morning had never brought good news to anyone. "Hel—*ahem*. Hello?" My voice was gone from staying up for three days straight, soaking myself in coffee to finish a commission for the West Hollywood Men's Chorus Annual Gala and Fundraiser. It was my own fault for putting Alistaire's book tour ahead of my own obligations, and I was paying the piper.

"Is this Mosby Leslie?" The unfamiliar voice sounded very formal.

I sat up in bed, bracing for something. My parents had died when I was in art school, and I was the only child of two only children. I'd already gone through some of the worst times in my life as I'd tried to figure out things at the tender age of twenty.

Was this an art buyer who didn't have a clock? It was six in the fucking morning, for god's sake. If it was, I vowed not to sell their client the toilet paper I wiped my ass on. People had no common sense these days.

"Yes. This is Mosby Leslie, and let me tell you that if you're calling to try to set up—"

"Mr. Leslie, are you the emergency contact for Alistaire Scott?"

That stopped me cold. "Yes."

"Mr. Leslie, this is Lieutenant Joe Norman from Chicago PD. I'm afraid I have some bad news, sir."

One-Mississippi... two-Mississippi... I was savoring the seconds before my world was blown apart.

"What's wrong with Alistaire?" My heart pounded. I could only assume the news was bad because of the hour of the call.

"I'm afraid Mr. Scott has drowned. His body was found at 31st Street Beach this morning. There was a note with your name and phone number inside a plastic bag in his coat pocket."

I glanced out the window next to our bed to see the sun was coming up, so I wasn't having a nightmare. Alistaire couldn't swim, which was why he never went to the cabin with me because he hated being near the water, and there was a small lake a little farther up the mountain. He wouldn't even go with me to the beach when I went to catch the sunrise.

"That makes no sense. Alistaire can't swim. What was he doing in the water in Chicago in March? Don't you people still have snow and ice on the ground?"

Spring had sprung in Southern California, but from what Alistaire had said when I'd spoken to him the previous night, lake-effect snows were coming overnight on the shores of Lake Michigan. It was why I'd returned to California after spending Valentine's Day in New York. I had no desire to feel the cold winds coming off the lake as they swept through Chicago during Alistaire's book-signing event in Wicker Park.

"That's the part we're hoping you can clear up for us, Mr. Leslie. You live in southern California, correct?"

Clearly, they'd looked me up before they'd called. What the fuck was going on?

"I do. I live here with Alistaire. He was on a book tour for his latest release. I just spoke to him last night. He was going to dinner with his agent, and then they were going to a jazz club. How the hell did he end up in the water?" It was more me thinking out loud than addressing the man's questions.

"The Coast Guard received a report of someone stealing a boat at Navy Pier. One of the security guards called it in, saying they believed some kids had stolen a vessel docked there. The owner was notorious for leaving an extra set of keys onboard, and the guard had seen the pontoon boat leaving the marina. It was heading east on Lake Michigan during a terrible windstorm. The Coast Guard went to look for the boat and found it abandoned. This morning, Mr. Scott's body washed up on 31st Street Beach, which is when we got the call."

Nothing was fitting together in my mind. "Are you telling me my partner stole a pontoon boat, took it for a joy ride on Lake Michigan at night during a windstorm, and ended up dead?"

"Yes."

Cut and dried.

My world was shattered.

Chapter One
Tyler Rockwell

April 2024

"Hi, Mrs. Mannon. Edina will be right with you. Have a seat, and I'll get you a cup of coffee."

"Thank you, dear. You keeping yourself out of trouble? Your mother was so worried about you"—she held her hand up to her mouth as if telling a secret—"when you were incarcerated." Her whisper echoed off the walls of the salon.

"Yes, ma'am." I went back to the kitchen where everything was located, filling a paper cup with coffee I hoped was scalding hot. She and Evelyn gave me the most shit out of everyone in town, though the others loved to remind me of things that happened while I was "gone"—as in, while I was in prison.

Yes, I did a stupid thing in high school. And it wasn't because I didn't have supervision as the son of a single mother—the prevailing theory around Foggy Basin.

Foggy Basin was the ultimate small town, and there wasn't much to do. The kids at the high school never understood me, the gay kid who loved makeup and painted nails.

I'd gone to a consolidated school district with kids from several other villages like Foggy Basin, and everyone had wanted to fit in. If one looked around the halls, they would've sworn we were a religious school with uniforms, but we weren't. Everyone copied everyone else regarding fashion, hair, and extracurricular activities. They'd all been afraid to stand out from the crowd.

Enter me—a bastard child born to be different, just like my mother. To say Marlena Rockwell was a free spirit was an understatement, and just like her, I followed no one. I loved makeup, fashion, and music of all kinds, and when I walked into a room, I wanted to be noticed. I was born to be a leader, Mom used to say, which may have been true until I fucked it up.

I carried the coffee to Mrs. Mannon on the tray Mom insisted I use with the sweeteners and creamers we had on hand for our clients. Mrs. Mannon picked up the small pitcher of creamer and sniffed it, her face morphing into an ugly scowl.

"That's sour, Tyler. You should always check the cream before you give it to the clients. Did your mother never teach you to return it to the refrigerator every time it's used?" I was surprised I had a tongue left with all the biting of it against all the bullshit shoveled at me from our clients.

"Mrs. Mannon, it's not cream. It's non-dairy vanilla spice creamer. We're out of regular cream, so use it or drink your coffee black. Don't give Tyler a hard time." Thank god Edina had come out from the back.

I turned to the reception desk to see Wendy Claymont waiting to pay for her color and cut, so I took the tray with me to check her out.

"Do you need any products today?" Edina had placed the ticket for Wendy on the desktop's keyboard, so I knew what services to charge for.

"I need some texturizer." Wendy smiled as she pulled out her credit card.

I bagged up our signature texturizer and handed it to her as I rang up the sale. Wendy left with a cheerful, "Have a great day."

"Ty?"

I turned toward the back of the salon to see my mother coming my way. She always directed a happy smile at me, but in my heart, I knew I didn't deserve it.

"Yeah, Mom?"

"Can you remove the foils and shampoo Bev Kyles for me?"

"Is she gonna grab my crotch again?" Beverly Kyles was newly divorced, and the last time I'd shampooed her, she'd grabbed my dick and stroked it over my apron and jeans. Unfortunately, it deflated further instead of springing to life. I hadn't told my mother about the encounter until a week after it happened. Mom had apologized, but it wasn't her apology to make.

"I talked to her about that, son. I told her I wouldn't continue to have her as a client unless she apologized to you and kept her hands to herself." Mom always took the bull by the horns.

I kissed Mom's cheek and went to her station to get Beverly Kyles. "Ms. Kyles, if you'll follow me."

The woman rose from Mom's chair, a look of dread on her face. "Tyler, I'm so sorry if I offended you last time."

If? Had she lost her fucking mind? "Ms. Kyles, I was highly offended. I was always taught to keep my hands to myself." Without a comment, she sat in the chair and I, not so gently, pulled out the foils, laughing to myself when she shrieked in discomfort.

After clearing the foils from the basin, I turned on the cold water, which was like ice. Ms. Kyles jumped when it hit her scalp to rinse the bleach. "Oh, is that too cold?"

There would be a special place in hell for me, but at that point, I didn't give a damn. I adjusted the water temperature to do as Mom asked. After shampooing the woman, I left her at the basin while I went to Mom's station. "You got the toner ready?"

"Did she apologize?"

"Define *apologize*." I reached for the toner Mom had just mixed. I didn't mind helping Mom when she needed an extra set of hands. Having learned barbering in prison prepared me for working in her salon, and I enjoyed being there.

There were a lot of difficult customers in the world, but none worse than inmates. Fuck up their hair, and nobody was as difficult to deal with as a pissed-off felon with nothing to lose.

"Let it go, Mom. She's got more money than sense. We're a for-profit business, so let her spend it here."

I took the tub of purple cream with me to the basin and began brushing the mixture onto Beverly's hair. I was a professional and could remain so, even though I didn't like the client. I'd watched Mom do it for years.

"Okay, Ms. Kyles. I'll be back in fifteen minutes to shampoo and condition your hair again, and then Marlena will be ready for your cut and style." I dried my hands and turned to walk away when the woman grabbed my ass. "Eep!"

I turned around, ready to say something when Edina walked over to the woman and grabbed her boob. "How do you like that?" Edina was giving the woman a death glare if I ever saw one.

"I'm not a lesbian!" Ms. Kyles looked scandalized, and I was trying like hell not to laugh.

"Well, how do you think Ty feels. He doesn't know you and he didn't invite your advances, Bev."

"I believe I'm the woman to turn him, Edina. I know Marlena would like grandchildren. One night with me, and Tyler will be chasing all the young ladies in town."

"How damn dumb are you, Beverly? Tyler is just fine the way he is. You really need to get some counseling. No wonder Andre Craig divorced you. You're a nymphomaniac! You can't keep your panties on, girl."

"Marlena! I demand—"

"Enough!" We all turned to see my mother had overheard the altercation. Her inner mama bear came to the surface in a hurry.

I walked away to let them figure it out. I went out the back door and sat at the table behind the shop to take a break. I'd picked up smoking in prison, but when I got out, Mom put her foot down that I had to quit, and I was so glad she had.

I closed my eyes to try to calm down. Letting some of those women rile me up was probably bad for my health.

"You wanna go to lunch?" I turned to see Alice Landing by the back door. She was a sweet girl around my age who Mom had hired about seven months prior, just before I got out of Folsom on early release. Alice was a blonde-haired, blue-eyed beauty with zero self-confidence.

Camila Ortiz walked outside behind her with a smirk. "Come on, handsome. Let's go get some tacos."

Camila's older brother owned a food truck that went from town to town in the area where we lived. It was Tuesday, which meant The Taco Wagon was in Foggy Basin by Veterans Park where they were hosting a spring break camp for school-age kids. Ramon's food was excellent, so it would be busy, but I liked to eat there because he was a really friendly guy.

"Sure. Let me grab my phone."

"No, don't go in there. Bev's still here, and your mother is chewing her ass out good. This will be the last time her butt hits Marlena's chair," Camila speculated.

I'd like to say I felt bad, but that would be a lie. That shit about *turning me*? I'd love to see her try.

Alice, Camila, and I walked over to Veterans Park. It was a nice day to be outside, and the park was busy with everyone taking advantage of the early spring breezes. Alice shared her latest man troubles, and Camila offered sage advice as a widow of four years who hadn't jumped back into the dating pool. "He's a mama's boy. Cut him loose now before you're too far down the road with him."

"What's that mean?" Alice asked the question I'd been thinking.

"It means before you fall in love with him, sweetheart. Trust me, it only gets worse if you end up in love with a mama's boy." Camila's eyes got that faraway look I'd seen a few times.

Camila's husband had been an airplane mechanic in the Air Force. They'd been stationed at Vandenberg in Southern California and had planned to start a family. He was killed in an accident involving an exploding tire on base, and Camila moved back to Foggy Basin to be closer to her family.

Her parents and brother all lived in Miller's Point—close but not *too* close. I understood her need for privacy completely.

"He's nice though. I mean, he's polite. He opens doors and says please and thank you. I don't think it's too much to ask that his mother not go on every date with us." Alice was so naïve it bordered on ridiculous. Unfortunately, I couldn't throw stones because I'd been much like her before prison.

"Girl, if Hector would have brought his mother on one date, I'd have cut that man loose in a heartbeat. You gotta put your foot down. I think it might be too late for you with Ryan." I thought Camila had a point, but then again, I'd never been in a relationship. What I had with my cell mate hadn't been anything like I hoped a relationship would be. It'd been Survival 101.

Alice looked at me with those big eyes. "What do you think, Ty? You're a guy."

I chuckled. "Not according to Beverly Kyles."

"Tyler don't let that bitch get to you. Your mother was rinsing her hair and giving her hell. She refused to give her a cut and told her not to call for another appointment. She told Beverly to be ready for our lawyer to call because you'd probably file a harassment lawsuit against her."

I laughed. "We don't have a lawyer."

Camila and Alice laughed with me. My mother was truly my champion.

We stewed over the extensive menu printed on a chalkboard attached to the side of the truck. When it was our turn, I ordered three beef barbacoa tacos with rice and beans, while the other two decided to share a three-enchilada platter.

"How you doin', Tyler?" Ramon gave me my change from our lunch even though I told him to keep it. My attitude was considerably better than when I'd left the shop because of the walk and the good company, so I sent my friends to get us a table while I waited for our orders.

"I'm good. I'm settling into the apartment over the shop, which is nice." I'd argued with Mom every day after the first week of living with her to let me move into the large studio apartment over the salon.

It had been sitting empty since Mom had bought the building from her old friend, Edith Rey. Mom had worked for Edith when I was growing up, and I'd considered Edith a grandmother figure. She'd died while I was in prison, and I missed her a lot.

"Yeah, I remember when Camila came back. Mom wanted her to move in with her and Dad, but Cam insisted she had to have her own space. I'm proud of her for standing her ground." I could see the admiration on Ramon's face.

"How about you? How's business?" Making small talk was still sort of new to me. There wasn't a lot of that in prison.

Words were transactional behind bars. *"Blow me, now." "I don't want to." Smack!* Done.

"Things are good, just like at the salon, from what Cam says. She also said your mother wants you close." *Understatement.*

"Smotheringly close. I get why but I need to figure things out for myself. She acts as though we haven't missed a step since I was that stupid seventeen-year-old kid who made a mistake. I grew up a lot in prison, but she thinks I'll still fuck up if she's not there to keep me out of trouble."

Ramon stepped out of the truck, leaving the grill to his assistant, German. "I know it's tough to get used to being on the outside again. Didn't your PO give you the name of a counselor? Even if it's not part of your parole agreement, I'd still take advantage of it. It helped German when he got out."

That surprised me, but I barely knew Ramon, and I knew nothing about German. He was a big guy—six-four or five, two-twenty-five, if I was guessing. German was a good-looking man of few words with long brown hair and a short beard. He always waved and smiled but didn't speak.

I nodded. "I, uh, I have a video call with my therapist on Friday. The parole board wanted in-person visits, but they couldn't find anyone nearby, and I don't have a license to drive anywhere. I won't be able to get it back until my parole ends in three years because my crime involved me driving a car."

I'd explained everything to my coworkers at the shop when I first started, but I could tell Camila, being the kind of person who wouldn't share my personal failings, hadn't told her brother my life story. It wasn't as if I cared. I was used to getting judged.

I was developing a thick skin when it came to people's suggestions for how I should live my life now that I was on the outside. Even Mom, sometimes.

"Come on, mi amigo. Let's go eat."

Ramon sat with us, and we all ate together, laughing at Ramon's stories about mishaps while starting his business. When we finished eating, I cleaned off the picnic table, and we said our goodbyes. As I was about to join the ladies in returning to the shop, Ramon stopped me. "Do you have appointments that can be booked, or are you an assistant at Shear Bliss?"

His hair was really short, so I wasn't sure what he was getting at. "I have my license to cut hair. Do you need a cut?"

Ramon rubbed his palm over his short buzz cut. "Not much there to cut. No, uh, German wants a trim, and he doesn't trust Cam. She threatened to cut it like mine when he falls asleep. No, he asked if you could do it."

"Sure. Have him call the shop when he's ready, and I'll be happy to do it." He'd be my first client since I got out and started working with Mom. I was really excited.

Chapter Two
Mosby Leslie

"*Fuck!*" I stared at my phone as though the text message would change, though I knew it wouldn't.

> We are unable to deliver to your current location. Your order may be picked up at our local locker at 333 Main Street, Foggy Basin, California. The locker number is twenty-three, and the combination is 014223. Thank you for your business.

I wanted to slam my phone against the exposed log wall at the far end of the kitchen, but a broken phone wasn't what I needed. I needed acrylic paints, brushes, cotton canvas, and plastic palettes since I was using acrylics instead of oil paints.

The list was long and tedious, and there were no art supply stores in town. I'd found what I needed without leaving the cabin, but now they couldn't—or wouldn't—come up the small mountain or tall hill to deliver the shit. Just fucking great.

Since I now had to go to town, I decided to inventory what I had on hand and make one big run. Grabbing a pad, I walked out to the barn where I had an extra freezer and storage shelves and started making a list of everything I needed—which was more than I'd anticipated.

I'd been holed up in the cabin my grandfather had given me after my parents died. Granddad had become my rock when my mom and dad died in a car accident. We got along very well until he passed away about three years ago. When he died, I was lost, once again. The cabin had become my safe haven after all the heartache I'd experienced, and I hated leaving it.

After Alistaire's death, I'd wanted to end my life. I'd been more broken than I believed possible, but being at the cabin surrounded by Granddad's things kept me from doing something I couldn't undo.

After arranging for Alistaire's body to be shipped from Chicago to a funeral home near his parents' home in Bel Air, I went to my studio with a bottle of vodka and drank. When that one was empty, I ordered a case. Then another, and then another.

Two weeks later, Alistaire's parents buried the man I'd been with for ten years. I didn't attend the family-only service, but I went to the cemetery and watched from afar, flask in hand.

I'd been attracted to Alistaire's unconventional spirit. He'd told me he didn't believe in marriage, and to a twenty-four-year-old kid, it wasn't a big deal. We'd bought a bungalow in WeHo and turned a back porch into a studio where we could work together.

Alistaire had been a writer. He'd been writing the next great American tome, and I was a painter working with oils. My art went relatively unnoticed—and unpurchased—so I gave drawing and painting classes at the West Hollywood Arts Center.

I was approached by the center director to rally some kids who attended the after-school program to create a kid-friendly mural to cover the graffiti on the back of the center. Natalie Wu, who later became my agent, saw the mural as we were painting it and stopped at the center to ask about the artist.

A month later, I had an agent, an advance to paint the mayor of West Hollywood's official portrait, and my career was on an upward trajectory. Alistaire's first novel was picked up by a publishing house in San Francisco around the same time, and he spent much of his time traveling between our little cottage in WeHo and the Bay area to work with his editor on changes to the manuscript to make a stand-alone novel into a three-book series that became a smashing success.

Funny story—once I'd moved to Foggy Basin, I stumbled into Books, Beans, and Buns for a coffee and decided to peruse the shelves. There, in the mystery section, were Alistaire's books, sending me into a spiral for a week.

Anyway, shortly after we were discovered, we moved into a larger house in Montecito where we had private studios and more rooms than we'd ever need. For the next several years, we were both insanely busy, traveling around the world for inspiration, often together but sometimes not. From the outside, it appeared as though we had the world by the ass, but the opposite was true.

Strange phone calls and text messages to Alistaire in the middle of the night should have been my first clue that all wasn't kosher between us, but I guess when one lodges their head so far up their own ass because they believe the sycophants around them, they deserve the shock of their lives to bring them back to reality. That was the way it happened to me, anyway.

Once I had my supply list together, I went out to Granddad's old Ford Bronco and put cloth grocery bags in the back seat. I wasn't a tree hugger—I just hated the plastic bags.

My pet squirrel, Barbara Bushy, sat on the rail of the back deck staring at me. I'd found her down by the gate that led to my driveway. She'd been injured, so I wrapped her in a towel and took her to Claws, Paws, and More, where the vet, Alex, checked the animal out and told me she was just stunned. She was a tough gal, just like the former first lady, thus the name, Barbara Bushy.

"I put your food out. I'll be back." I truly wondered if I was losing my mind. Talking to a squirrel that kept coming around because I'd taken it to a doctor and continued to put out food for wouldn't go over well in any mental health assessments.

I hopped into the Bronco and grinned when it started on the first try. I'd had a local mechanic install a new engine a month earlier because I didn't want to let it go. It was the most dependable thing in my life right now, and I couldn't let her die.

I made the thirty-minute drive down the mountain with the window down so the nice early spring breeze could cool the Bronco. The A/C had died a long time ago. It was a beautiful part of the country, and if I had to live like a hermit somewhere, Foggy Basin wasn't a bad spot.

My hair was out of control because I hadn't cut it or the beard in a year. The beard hid my face, which was exactly what I wanted. There had been a recent article in an online gossip rag about my disappearance from the LA art scene since the death of my long-term partner. The speculation was that I'd moved to Europe to escape the memories. My preference was let it stay that way.

I passed Lover's Butte, not surprised to see several cars parked there in the daylight. It was a great place to leave a vehicle while hiking in the area, and at night, it filled up with cars full of couples wanting to watch the sunset and get a little frisky if the mood struck. I was jealous of all of them.

When I braked at the stop sign leading to the small town, I grabbed a rubber band from the ashtray and secured the top of my hair to keep it out of my face before parking in the public lot across from the stores on Main Street.

I crossed the street and headed toward the post office where the package lockers were located. The nosy mailman was making his way down the street, so I wanted to hurry. He asked far too many questions for my liking.

I found locker twenty-three and punched in the code, hearing the tumblers turn before the door opened. Inside were two large boxes, so I pulled them out and carried them across the street to the Bronco. Once I had them in the back, I grabbed the grocery sacks and crossed the street again to go to the small grocery store across the alley from the hair salon on the corner.

For a split second I considered going in to get a haircut but abandoned that idea just as quickly. When I walked by the window with the fancy *Shear Bliss* sign painted in eggplant and silver, I saw just how damn scary I looked in my paint-splattered pants and hole-riddled T-shirt, and I laughed.

All my Armani suits and Gucci shoes were back in Montecito in the closet I'd once shared with Alistaire. His things had been sent to his family after I'd sobered up following news of his death. I bought out his half of the house and had his box-filled Ferrari Purosangue picked up and towed to his parents' estate in Bel Air.

Not dealing with the Scotts after Alistaire's death had been my goal. They blamed me for Alistaire not continuing his PhD. in literature and pursuing a profession more noble than fiction writing. However, I wouldn't have been able to live with myself if I hadn't told them their son had died. Even I wasn't that cold-hearted.

After I broke the news to them, they accused me of being responsible for Alistaire's suicide, though the authorities had changed the cause of death to an accident. I only discovered the change when I received updated copies of the death certificate to close out our joint accounts per the domestic partnership agreement we'd put in place when we bought the Montecito house.

Of course, the authorities were aware it wasn't an accident—they'd found the note in his pocket that said he was sorry, but he couldn't go on without the love of his life. He'd listed my name and number in the note as a contact, and they'd jumped to the conclusion it was me and we'd broken up, which was why I'd gotten the call. I had a feeling his parents pulled some strings to have the death certificate revised to keep their son's demise from becoming a scandal.

I only met the Scott's face-to-face once, and they hated me immediately. Because of that horrific birthday dinner gone wrong, Alistaire hadn't spoken to them for the rest of our time together before his death. If believing it was my fault Alistaire killed himself helped them find closure, so be it. Tariq Jackson would forever remain blameless.

"Excuse me." I turned to see a woman behind me, pointing to the row of shopping carts I was blocking. I recognized her as the woman who owned the salon. She had kind eyes.

I stepped aside and allowed her to take a cart. I'd once again been lost in my thoughts and had inconvenienced someone else.

"I'm sorry."

"No worries." She gave a friendly smile and went into the store. I grabbed a cart and followed behind.

My mind wandered back to my life before Foggy Basin. Every time I caught Alistaire cheating, he'd said I was an inconvenience because I believed in monogamy. When he met Tariq, and I learned about it after Alistaire's death, I wondered if he'd had a point.

I snapped out of it and went on with my shopping. I'd been missing fresh produce. I'd tried to plant a little garden patch the previous spring when I first arrived at the cabin, but the yard was too shady for it to take off. I couldn't justify cutting down a huge Arroyo Willow so I could plant a patch of vegetables. It seemed selfish.

I loaded the cart with tomatoes, carrots, corn on the cob, and other seasonal favorites. I'd taken an online canning course when I'd planted the garden last year, optimistically believing I'd be awash in fresh vegetables by the fall. That didn't happen, but if I could secure some canning jars and lids, I could can some of the fresh produce I was stacking in my cart and put the jars in the root cellar to have over the winter. It was more homestead-ish than I wanted to be, but if I wanted veggies later in the fall, it was an option.

I gathered all the supplies I needed for a couple of months and went to the checkout. The place was relatively deserted, which suited me just fine.

The clerk, a tall, older man with a pinched face and a pointy nose glared at me. "You got money to pay for this before I start ringing it?"

Yes, it was a large order, but fuck him. I reached into my pocket to get my wallet and found it missing.

"Crap. I'll be right back. I forgot my wallet in the truck."

I hurried out of the store and across the alley, winding up in front of the salon. I glanced through the picture window and came to a screeching halt. Inside, standing at the register and talking to a woman with long hair was a gorgeous young man.

I stared at him for a moment. When he glanced up, he smiled, which made my heart pound. He was more beautiful than I'd first thought, and his smile...? Magnificent.

My face flushed at being caught gawking, but hell, I'd never seen such a striking creature. I turned to hurry away before he came after me with a broom, and I caught the toe of my sneaker on something, taking me down to the sidewalk with a—

Chapter Three
Tyler

"Your mom seems so happy to have you back in town." It was Tricia Sykes, the dispatcher at the sheriff's office just down the street. She'd just had a baby and wanted her hair trimmed before she went back to work.

Tricia didn't strike me as malicious with her comment as others had been, smiling at me while I processed her credit card. At least there was someone decent besides the folks at Shear Bliss.

"I'm definitely happy to be here." The receipt spewed from the machine, so I grabbed a pen and a clipboard, sliding the ticket under the bar for Tricia to sign.

"You should meet my brother, Jeremy. He's in town for a few weeks helping Lance do some repairs at the house. Maybe you wanna come over—"

I glanced out the window and saw a man who appeared to be living on the street. Our eyes locked, and his were the most vivid blue I'd ever seen.

The man had a wild dark-blond beard and long messy hair, the top of which was pulled up with a rubber band. His clothes were old and had seen better days, but those eyes...

Suddenly, he jerked and turned to hurry away before he completely disappeared.

"Oh damn!" I rushed from behind the counter and ran outside, finding the man face down on the sidewalk. *Fucking hell!* He'd tripped over our broken step.

I rushed over and gently turned him onto his back. He was breathing, though I believed him to be unconscious. His left cheek was scraped and his nose was bleeding. I quickly took off my apron and gingerly wiped the cracked pieces of concrete away before holding the apron under his nose to try to catch some of the blood.

"Oh, dear god! What happened?" I glanced up to see Mom standing on the top step.

"He fell over this broken stair. I told you to call someone to get it fixed."

I didn't know how to repair concrete. I could hang things or change lightbulbs, but that was the extent of my home-repair knowledge. Cars? Even less.

"Blasted! I forgot all about it, Ty. Should I call the ambulance?"

The stranger opened his eyes. "Where...? What...? What happened?"

Close up, the blue eyes left me speechless. Mom nudged my back with her knee, so I shook off my fascination. "You fell and hit your head, I'm afraid."

"My head?"

"I'm so sorry. Yes, you tripped over our—" And there was my mother admitting fault right off the bat!

"Mom! Get the man a wet cloth."

All we needed was a trip-and-fall lawsuit. I tossed my bloody apron over the broken step to hide it and helped the man sit up. "Do you hurt anywhere?"

"I hurt everywhere. I just fell." He wasn't nasty about it, just stating a fact and staring at me as though he thought I was stupid.

"We have a volunteer fire department and paramedic unit. Do you want us to call them?" Mom knelt next to me. "Is there someone we can call for you? Where do you live?"

"I— I live in Montecito."

"I'm calling Sheriff West. I think he needs to be checked out by the paramedics. What's your name, honey?"

The man seemed a little put off by Mom's clipped tone if his scowl was any proof, so I did my best to smooth it. "I'm Tyler. That's Marlena. We want you to get checked out. Is it okay if we call the sheriff? He'll call the paramedics to be sure you're okay."

"I'm okay—" Suddenly, the stranger sprang to his feet.

"Wait! You might have a concussion or something!" I stood to run after him.

"No police!" He stumbled a bit, but I caught him before he fell.

I was no lawyer, but I knew that if someone was injured on your property, you were liable and could be sued. I definitely didn't want that to happen to Mom. She was just starting to make a profit at the shop after taking out a second mortgage to pay my attorney when I was arrested as an accessory to armed robbery.

I'd vowed to pay back every penny Mom spent trying to keep me out of prison, though it had all been for nothing.

She'd gone above and beyond her motherly obligations when I fucked up, and I would do everything in my power to repay her. I wouldn't let anything bad happen to her, either.

"Okay, okay. No cops. I actually agree with you on that one. My apartment is on the second floor over the shop. Will you consent to coming upstairs with me so I can watch you for a little while? I'll fix you something to eat, and you can shower if you'd like. I'll wash your clothes for you."

His face screwed up for a moment before he nodded. At least I said something right.

"Okay. Good. Let's go around back to the separate entrance. I need to let Mom know what's going on, so have a seat on the stairs. I'll help you climb them in a minute."

He nodded and went to the stairway while I hurried around the corner and into the shop. Mom was standing at the reception desk on the phone, so I went to the back and grabbed a bucket to fill with water to rinse off the steps and sidewalk. Nobody needed to see blood in front of Shear Bliss.

Just as I stepped outside, Reuben Bennett, the mailman, walked by and handed me the mail. "I saw that guy fall. Is he okay? You know, I've mentioned to your mother about fixing that step more than once. She should talk to Jack

Hulbert at Nuts and Bolts. I'm sure he'd know someone to do the job."

Just what we needed—the nosy fucking mailman as a witness to the guy falling in front of our shop. Why were the fates conspiring against me?

"He's fine. Nothing to worry about. Do you know him?"

"Name's Leslie, I believe. I believe he lives out in the woods somewhere higher up the hill, but the mailbox is outside a locked gate so I don't know what the house looks like. Mail comes to a Moslie Consolidated, LLC. I see him around town every few months, but he's not very friendly. Might be crazy. You know, some homeless have mental illnesses that make them violent. You better be careful with him."

I rolled my eyes so hard it was surprising they didn't stick that way. "I, uh, I think the term is now unhoused, Mr. Bennett, and we don't know anything about him, so let's not form a negative opinion off the bat. I don't think he's dangerous, but I'll be careful. Thank you."

I took the mail and the bucket and returned inside. Mom was back at her station with her next client, so I walked over, leaning to speak into her ear. "I have the guy waiting for me on the steps. I'll take him upstairs to my place to keep an eye on him for a while so we know if he's injured badly. I'll feed him and wash his clothes. Let's keep our fingers crossed that he doesn't find a lawyer and end up owning the shop. I'll come back and close things up tonight. What time's your last appointment?"

"Do you trust him in your apartment alone?" My mother's face... She was worried, like always, and it made me chuckle.

"Mom, aside from the frame you gave me with the picture of us when I got out of Folsom, I can't imagine I've got anything worth any money that he might steal."

Mom blushed, which was cute. I gave her a hug before I left.

When I walked around the side of the building, I saw Leslie—if that was his name—leaning his head against the railing with his eyes closed. I had no clue how old he was, but I hoped that allowing him into my apartment wouldn't lead to a squatting situation.

"Mr. Leslie, can you make it up the stairs?"

His eyes popped open, and he sat up, rubbing his face. His nails were relatively clean for someone who lived on the streets. I hated that the old stereotype of someone foraging through a trash can was the first thought I'd had. I dealt with my own stigmas. I shouldn't assign them to others.

"Yes. If you have some pain relievers, I'd appreciate them. I might have sprained my wrist, but I'm not sure." He was holding his wrist and rubbing it, so I helped him stand and guided him up the stairs. When we reached the top, I flipped the corner of the rug and grabbed the key to unlock the door.

"It's not much—" What the hell was I saying to a man who seemingly didn't have housing?

I helped Mr. Leslie inside and onto a chair at my small kitchen table. "Can I get you something to eat? I have stuff for sandwiches if you're hungry."

"Just water, please."

I nodded before hurrying to my kitchenette and opening the fridge to grab a bottle of water. I reached into a cabinet and picked up a bottle of pain relievers, shaking out two and taking them to Mr. Leslie. "I'll be right back with a couple of sandwiches. Do you like ham or turkey? Oh, how about cheese?"

"Really, it's unnecessary. I'll be fine. I've already taken up enough of your time." He took the pills and drank the water before trying to stand, only to stumble.

"You better sit down, Mr. Leslie. We might need to take you to the urgent care in Miller's Point. I think you might have a concussion. Maybe no food yet. Let me get some ice for your wrist."

An hour later, Mr. Leslie threw up the water and pain relievers, so I had Mom drive us to the clinic in the next town. They diagnosed him with a mild concussion and x-rayed his wrist. Thankfully, nothing was broken.

"He needs to be watched for the next twenty-four hours. If his headache gets worse or if he throws up again, he'll need to be seen by a doctor at Hartsville Mercy. We can't do a head CT here." The nurse practitioner who ran the clinic was very nice, but she seemed quite concerned, which had me equally worried.

"He can come stay at my house," Mom piped up.

"No, no. He can stay at my place. You've got a full day tomorrow, so you can't stay up all night. I have no appointments. I can stay up with him and make sure he's comfortable."

We didn't need an unhoused man dying after a fall at our shop. I was trying to get on my feet and take the burden of worry off my mother, not add more to it.

Mr. Leslie was showering when my phone rang. I didn't recognize the number, but I had to answer because my parole officer could call any time and I was required to speak with them. "Tyler Cromwell."

"Hi, Tyler. It's German Belmonte calling from Ramon's phone. He got your number from Camila and told me to call for an appointment to have my hair trimmed. Is this a bad time?"

My first client... "Hi, German. How are you?"

"I'm fine. Can you fit me in sometime this week?"

I wanted to laugh. I had no appointments anytime in the near or far future. Nobody in town would let me touch their hair except to shampoo it, and some wouldn't even let me do that.

"I, uh, how about Friday? Morning or afternoon?" I grabbed a pen and a piece of paper from the drawer, ready to write down my first-ever appointment to get paid for doing what I'd trained to do in prison. I didn't even have an appointment book.

"Uh, afternoon is better. We close the truck at three, so after that would be great." German's voice was deep and quiet.

"How about three forty-five? That way you can clean up the truck first."

"Yeah, yeah, that works. I just want a trim, so it shouldn't take long."

"Of course, German. No worries. I'll shampoo your hair so you can come straight from the park. I'll see you Friday afternoon."

"Thanks, Tyler. I'm looking forward to it."

I couldn't keep the smile from my face. *My first customer...*

Chapter Four
Mosby

Why the hell am I pretending to be in pain? And seriously? Sticking my finger down my throat? I've lost my mind.

Yes, the young man was very pretty. Yes, he had a very welcoming face, and that smile nearly did me in.

Yes, I was letting him draw his own conclusions about me because it seemed like he'd put me out of his modest apartment if I said I had more money than I could ever spend, a six-bedroom home, and a mountain cabin.

Looking around the tiny space he called home, I could see any commentary from me about his living arrangements would be demeaning and arrogant. Hell, the way I looked, I doubted he'd believe me if I told him I was a world-famous painter.

I walked out of the small bathroom having just taken a shower. My face looked busted as fuck, but maybe that was a good thing. It would make me less recognizable, not that I thought anyone in Foggy Basin would recognize me.

I went to the small bedroom and pulled on Tyler's T-shirt and lounge pants—which hit me just below the knees because he was shorter than me—and I walked into the open-plan kitchen and living room where he was finishing a phone call. His smile was a mile wide.

"Ah! How was your shower? Do you want to chance eating a sandwich? Maybe half? I'm sure you must be hungry. Maybe some soup? Mom makes great chicken soup, and I'm sure she has some in the freezer. I know it's not really soup weather any longer, but it might be lighter on your stomach. She just lives a block away. I can be back in five minutes."

Tyler ushered me over to the couch where he'd placed another bottle of water, the remote for the small television resting on a milk crate, and a box of tissues on the old oak coffee table. It was thoughtful.

"Soup would be good."

I hoped if I limited my responses, I wouldn't say something that would ruin our time together. Having the sweet guy around made me feel better than I had in a year.

"Okay. I'll be right back. Make yourself at home, please."

I nodded, and he rushed out the door, his feet pounding down the wooden stairs. I stood and looked out the window, watching him run down the sidewalk. I walked over to the door and stepped out on the small porch. My truck was still in the parking lot across from the shops on Main Street, which was good. I was guessing my grocery cart had been emptied while one of the cashiers cursed me under their breath.

"How long are you going to play this game? What *is* the game?" I was talking out loud to myself without the cover of Barbara Bushy, but maybe I was the only one who could talk some sense into me.

"Who am I hurting? One night in town, and then I'll return to the cabin for another three months."

I stepped back inside the apartment and glanced around. There was one picture on the wall. I walked over to take it in, seeing Tyler with his mother, Marlena. She really must have had Tyler when she was young. She looked younger than me in the photo.

It appeared they were standing in front of the small Kia they'd used to take me to the clinic in Miller's Point, but the background in the photo didn't look familiar. It was more industrial. There was a chain link fence with razor wire at the top, so I had no idea where they were or why it was so secure.

They were both smiling, so it must have been a happy occasion. I vaguely remembered those with my own parents.

The apartment had decent furniture, though none of it was new. Everything was clean and tidy, which was more than I could say for the cabin. Since I'd started playing around with acrylics, I'd given up on keeping things neat.

I really had let myself go to hell. I'd shampooed my hair in his shower, and Tyler had left a comb, but instead of using it, I balled it up into the rubber band I'd had in it earlier.

I searched for my paint-splattered jeans and ragged T-shirt, hoping my truck and cabin keys were still inside. I hadn't locked the truck, and those supplies I'd picked up at the locker area by the post office were inside.

Just as I found the pocket doors hiding the stacked washer-dryer unit, the front door opened. "Mr. Leslie?"

I hurried down the short hallway to the living room and slowed, holding onto the wall. "I'm here."

"Are you okay?" His face showed concern.

"Used the bathroom."

Tyler nodded before he went to the kitchen area, so I followed him. "You live here alone?"

"I just moved up here. I lived with Mom after I—when I got back to town. That was a little more mothering than I wanted, so I moved in here, and I'm renting from her. Why don't you take a seat while I get this ready for you? I'm not really a cook, but I can heat things up."

I grunted like the rude bastard I could be, according to my late partner, Alistaire. Tyler had already decided I was living on the streets, so what was the harm in letting him believe it a little longer?

I picked up the empty bowl from the chicken noodle soup he'd heated for me. It'd been delicious, which was a surprise. It was better than anything I'd had in Los Angeles, though I hadn't been there in a year.

I'd hired a private security company to check the Montecito house daily, so I had no worries. They were paid by automatic debit from a business account I'd established after Alistaire died. I used it to pay expenses from his estate and for things I needed that couldn't be traced to me at the cabin. It was convenient and kept my identity a secret, just as it was designed to do.

"I'll get that, Mr. Leslie." Tyler was in the living room on a laptop. I had no idea what he was doing, but more importantly, how did he know my last name?

"Is that my name? How did you find out?" I might be pretending not to remember things, but now I wondered if I *was* concussed.

"Reuben Bennett, the mailman, said he thought that was your name. Is it not?" Tyler walked over to where I stood by the sink.

I swallowed. "I don't know. I don't remember. Where are my clothes?"

"Oh! Sorry. They're in the washer. They'll be dry in a while." He went to the washer and pulled out my things. The clank of keys startled him. He reached into the washer drum, pulling out the small keyring holding two keys that I'd had in my pocket.

Tyler held them up. "Do you know what these are to? Do you know where you found them?" He had a skeptical eyebrow aimed in my direction that I didn't like, but honestly, he didn't know me from a signpost.

"I don't remember them specifically, but they seem familiar. Do you think I'm a thief?" I took them from his hand and stared at them.

"I'm sorry, Mr— What should we call you?" His face was so sweetly sincere that I wanted to kiss him. He had not one evil bone in his body. What was his story? Where had he been before he'd returned to Foggy Basin?

Finally, I relented. "Call me Leslie." It was a half-truth, anyway.

"Okay, Leslie. How about we get you settled in my bedroom? I'll wake you up every hour or so, and if you have a headache, I'll give you a pain reliever. If you feel nauseous, I can get a bucket when I go down to the shop to lock up. I just changed my bedding this morning, unless you'd rather stay here on the couch. It was in the shop until I needed it up here, but I just put the slipcover on it. Either way is fine. It's up to you."

"Your bed!" That came out too fast. "I mean, it's kind of bright in here. I believe I'd rest better in your room."

Where I drew that witty conclusion, I had no idea. I'd glanced around his bedroom when I changed clothes. It was very neat, and there were black-out shades on the windows.

"Damn. I didn't think about that. I was Googling the symptoms of a concussion, so I'd know what to watch for.

It mentioned that a dark room was best. Let's get you set up back here before I run down and close the shop for the day."

I nodded and followed him down the hallway. Tyler turned down the bed and extended a hand for me to climb in, so I did. It was a nice mattress, though it was only a full-size bed. Mine at the cabin was a queen because that was all that would fit in the loft. The mattress in Montecito was a California king—the same one I'd shared with Alistaire since we'd bought the house. I hadn't even considered changing it, even though I was sure that after a year it no longer smelled like him.

Once Tyler had both pillows under my head and the sheet and thin quilt folded over me, he gave me a kind smile. "I won't be long. Do you need anything?"

Guilt slid down my spine at my deceptive behavior, but there was so much to learn about the young guy that I couldn't walk away yet. The last three years of our relationship, Alistaire and I hadn't had sex—well, with each other. I'd had my hand, and he'd had half of LA.

We occasionally went out together at the insistence of both our agents to keep our faces relevant, but we mostly lived separate lives. Tyler Rockwell was the first person I'd met who'd piqued my interest in years.

"I'll be fine. I just need a nap."

Tyler nodded. "I'll be back in about an hour."

He walked out, pulling the bedroom door closed with him. I put my keys on the nightstand and noticed a notebook, so being the nosy bastard I was, I picked it up. Flipping open the cardboard cover, I saw a folded piece of paper and opened it.

It was a list of typed questions. I glanced at the first page of the notebook to see neatly printed answers corresponding to the questions.

> 1. *What is the most important lesson you've learned due to your incarceration?*

That was interesting. Tyler had been incarcerated. My god, how old had he been and what crime had he committed? I couldn't imagine that beautiful young man doing harm to anyone on the face of the earth. I moved the paper to see the handwritten answer corresponding to the question.

> 1. *After making a stupid mistake as a seventeen-year-old kid just trying to fit in with anyone, I've realized I allowed myself to be influenced by people who didn't have my best interests at heart. Through counseling in Folsom, I've learned to be more observant and cautious when meeting new people. Any new friends I make will be carefully*

vetted before I begin to trust them and take them into my confidence.

I was guessing that pretending to have a concussion and not remembering my name would be a big no-no in the trust and confidence department.

Shit...

Chapter Five
Tyler

I entered the salon through the back door, listening to see if anyone else was still inside. When I was met with silence, I hurried to grab the broom, turning on the hair vac we had in the front of the salon. I quickly swept the floor and emptied the trash from everyone's stations.

There was an empty station that would be mine if I ever had a client. Actually, I had just acquired a client, hadn't I?

German Belmonte was coming in on Friday at three forty-five for a trim. I opened the drawer to admire the scissors and razors Mom had bought me when I was released. My initials were embossed in gold on the case that held them all. I was finally going to get to use them, and my heart was nearly beating out of my chest.

I finished mopping the floor and double-checked the door to be sure it was locked. Mom had flipped the sign when she left for the day, so I pulled the shade and turned off the lights. I went to the kitchen and grabbed a bucket to take upstairs with me for Leslie in case he felt sick to his stomach again.

I locked the back door and headed up the stairs to my place. I let myself in and listened. All was quiet.

The door to my bedroom was open, so I tip-toed down the short hall and stuck my head inside the room. Leslie was asleep on his back, and he'd kicked off the covers. I stepped closer and placed the bucket beside the bed, hoping he wouldn't need it.

I stared at him for a moment, his chest rising and falling easily. My sleep pants were too short on him, as was the T-shirt, but it did give me a nice peek at toned abs and an enticing happy trail.

"God, I really need to get laid." It came out without me realizing I'd said it out loud.

"Happy to oblige." I glanced up to see Leslie's eyes were open, and he was watching me stare at him. My face immediately heated.

"Sorry, uh, thinking out loud. Anyway, how are you? I brought a bucket if you feel sick. It's there on the floor by the nightstand." I turned to walk out of the room to make myself a bed on the couch.

"Where will you sleep?"

I turned to face him, seeing he was sitting up, his hair a messy pile on top of his head. "Couch is fine for me. I can trim your hair and beard if you'd like. I'm a barber." I had the license to prove it.

Leslie chuckled. "No thanks." He then rolled over with his back to me. I took that to mean he was going back to sleep, so I stopped in the hall and grabbed a set of sheets and an extra pillow. I checked the thermostat to see it was at seventy-two degrees, and I made a bed on the couch. I went to the small kitchen and grabbed a timer shaped like a chicken, setting it for an hour before I sacked out on the couch. It was going to be a long night.

Hour One—

The alarm startled me, and it took a moment to remember why I'd set it. I then remembered Leslie, so I hopped up and went to my bedroom where he was sleeping peacefully.

I touched his shoulder, tapping until those blue eyes met mine. "Yes?"

"I'm just waking you to see that you're okay."

I saw the flash of annoyance cross his face. "Unless you're going to pleasure me in some fashion, just make sure I'm still breathing."

I found his snarky response funny and wished I could return it in kind. "How do I know you're not in a coma if I don't wake you?"

Leslie studied me for a moment before he smirked. "You could climb in with me. If I stop breathing, you'll be the second to know."

I rolled my eyes and went back to the couch.

Hour Two—

There was no need to wake Leslie—he used the bathroom and woke me. He walked into the living room and gave me a sarcastic two-thumbs-up as the timer rang on the coffee table. I rolled over and went back to sleep.

Hour Six—

I slept through hours three through five because I forgot to set the timer. I got up to use the bathroom and make some coffee and stuck my head in the bedroom to see Leslie with *my* journal on the bed next to him. He was asleep, and the book was open with a pencil cradled in the crease.

I walked further into the room to see he'd sketched a picture. I walked around the bed to get a closer look, seeing it was me asleep on the couch. At the bottom of the picture, he'd written two sentences.

> *Don't quit your day job. You'd make a terrible nurse.*

I laughed out loud, and Leslie jerked awake. I wanted to chastise him for reading the journal I was tasked to write in for my therapy call later in the week, but I'd left it on the nightstand. Natural curiosity would have had me picking it up, too.

"I'm sorry I forgot to set the alarm. Obviously, you're still alive." I closed the journal and put it on top of the dresser.

"You're not upset with me for invading your privacy?" He seemed perplexed at me for not yelling about him looking at my journal.

"I left it out. How can I complain about you reading it when it was right there. I learned to pick my battles when I was in prison." Man, did I ever.

"How long were you there?" Leslie sat up and twisted his legs like a pretzel, so I sat down on the end of the bed to mirror him.

"I got arrested at seventeen for driving the getaway car in an armed robbery of a liquor store in Miller's Point. I became friends with a group of kids there who hung out at the arcade downtown. One of them ran out of money and said he needed a ride to the ATM, so the four of us got into my car, and I drove them to the liquor store. I thought there was an ATM inside that they would use, so I waited. When they ran out, one of them waving a knife, I was in shock. Jerry held the knife to my neck and told me to drive. I did—right to the sheriff's office."

I reached up and pulled down the collar of my T-shirt. "I got this when I laid on the horn and a deputy came out. We were all tried as adults because we were seventeen and eighteen, and I was sentenced to eight years as an accessory to armed robbery. I served five years and am on parole for three. I was granted early release six months ago, right before Thanksgiving."

There was no reason to lie about my past, even to a stranger whose business it *wasn't*. I was sure I'd be explaining myself for the rest of my life, but as I'd heard more than once, if you can't do the time, don't do the crime.

Leslie stared at me. "You drove the armed robbers to the sheriff's office and honked the horn?" He started laughing, which lit up his whole face in a very pleasant way. I was sure under all that hair was a very handsome man.

"I thought maybe it would go in my favor. It got a year shaved off my sentence and went over well with the parole board. The other three are still in prison, as far as I know. We were each sent to different prisons throughout the state, and we can't be in contact, which is fine with me."

"Were they close friends?" Leslie seemed intrigued by my story.

I chuckled. "I'd known them for about a month before it happened. They'd grown up together, and I didn't like the kids I went to school with. It's a typical bully story, but when I met those guys, they seemed cool with me. I was a naïve idiot back then. I was the makeup-and-nail-polish-wearing gay kid who didn't fit in and wanted desperately to find a place where I could."

"Ah. I've been down that road myself. So, how bad was prison?"

The alarm on my phone went off—thankfully—so I needed to get my ass in the shower to get to work. I'd used the kitchen alarm to wake me hourly so I didn't have to mess up the alarm setting on my phone. It was easier to use the plastic chicken alarm than fuck around with my phone.

"That's a story for another time. I gotta get to the salon. Will you be okay here today while I work? I'll come up when I get a break." I was oddly not nervous about leaving him in my space. He'd already seen my journal, so everything else was ordinary. No big surprises.

"I, uh, yeah. I'll be fine, thanks." He sounded unsure.

"Do you still have a headache?" I had pain relievers, but if he had a headache, I was going to suggest going to the hospital like the nurse practitioner at the clinic had advised.

"No. Head's just fine. Memories are coming back. I'll just get out of your hair. It was nice to meet you."

I'd put his clothes on the chair in the corner before I lay down last night, so he was ready to go. "There're your clothes. Do you remember where you live?"

Leslie's eyes studied the gingham plaid sheets for a moment before he grinned. "Yeah. I live up the mountain. I remembered when I woke up." He wore a sheepish grin, which was too damn cute for my own good.

"Well, okay then. Uh, I didn't find underwear in your clothes. Do you need some clean ones? How about an ice pack? You've got quite a scrape on your cheek. Uh, let me call my mom to come open the salon for the others. I'll get you a care package ready to take with you. How, uh, I can have Mom drive you home. I don't have a license any longer."

He tilted his head. "How do you get around?"

I giggled, which was embarrassing. "I walk. I'm saving to buy a bike. I won't get my license back for a long time. Everything I need is along that one street." I pointed toward the window that faced Main Street.

"Ah. Okay then. I'll come into the salon and say goodbye."

I nodded and hurried into my closet to grab clothes for the day. I rushed through my shower and then dressed, hurrying to get downstairs so I didn't have to bug Mom.

I quickly went through the cabinets and fridge, pulling together some ingredients for sandwiches, fruit, chips, a plastic bag with ice, and a dish towel for him to make an icepack for his face. I put everything, including a few bottles of water, into a small cooler I used when I went to the farmers' market with Mom outside of town. I could get another one the next time we went to the big box store in Hartsville.

"Okay, here you go. Keep the cooler. Uh, don't forget the keys there," I pointed to the counter where I'd placed the two keys on the little ball chain he'd had in his pocket.

"Yeah, thanks a lot for everything." He sipped his coffee as he stared at me.

I still had a baseball in my gut about his accident, so I decided just to ask him, face-to-face. "Are you going to sue us? Mom paid for the trip to the clinic, and if any follow-up is necessary, we'll cover that too."

He stared at me like I'd sprouted a second head. "Are you being nice because you're afraid I'll sue you?"

Was he mad? "Not entirely. I mean, Mom did so much for me when I went to prison, I guess I'm just trying to pay it forward. I don't know how to fix the step, and she was supposed to call someone to do it, but she forgot. I love her, but she can be a little flaky at times. I should have followed up on it myself."

"Pay it forward, huh? Well, all I have to pay forward is heartache. Give me a piece of paper and I'll sign a waiver that lets you and your mother off the hook. I won't sue you. You have my word."

I did as he asked, and he scrawled out a note to that effect, signing *Leslie* at the bottom. I glanced over it and folded it, sliding it into my pocket to give to Mom.

"Thank you. I hope you recover fast, and again, I'm sorry you tripped. Maybe when you come to town again, we could have lunch at Pints 'n Pool. They have great burgers. I think you and I could be friends."

I didn't expect his hysterical laughter.

Chapter Six
Mosby

I got dressed in my own clothes and grabbed the keys to my truck and the cabin. I couldn't tell if I was pissed that Tyler had only been nice to me out of fear of being sued or if I was sad to leave the sweetest guy I'd ever met behind. Maybe a little of both?

I grabbed the cooler he'd thoughtfully put together, and then I went down the stairs. I'd planned to stop by Shear Bliss to say goodbye to Tyler's mother but decided the waiver was enough. It gave the Rockwells the closure they needed, and I could drive the extra ten miles to Miller's

Point or even to Hartsville for groceries. I never had to go to Foggy Basin again.

Luckily, my truck was untouched in the parking lot, so I hopped in. It was warm inside because we were having an unseasonably warm spring, but there was nothing in the boxes I'd picked up the previous day that would have spoiled. The groceries I'd left behind, however, would have been a different story.

I drove out of the parking lot and made the left down Main Street to head back to the cabin. I could go to Miller's Point in the morning to get produce and canning jars if I was feeling ambitious.

Once home, I parked in the garage and took the supplies to my studio. I scanned the half-painted landscapes tilted against the walls. They'd helped me through some really rough times, but they were all amateurish, more paint-by-numbers than actual paintings. They'd suited their purpose of taking my mind off things that were painful at the time, but those canvases were meant for better things.

I collected them and took them out into the front yard, using sticks to prop them up to make my job easier. I went out to the shed where I stored larger supplies and rooted around until I found the primer and a four-inch sponge paintbrush. I stopped by the workbench, grabbed a block of sandpaper, and prepared to go to work.

Barbara Bushy hopped up on the porch railing, staring at me. "I told you I'd come back." I poured some of the gesso into an aluminum pan. I glanced down at my old jeans and laughed. Poor Tyler had tried to get the paint out of them, but some of the stains were a year old. I couldn't remember ever washing them.

I glanced toward the porch railing, seeing Bushy still there watching me. "You know what I miss? You'll never guess. Turpentine. I miss the smell of turpentine."

Bushy jumped off the railing onto the porch floor, scampering over to the stairs. I picked up the sandpaper and walked to the first canvas, running my hand over it to see how rough it was, and started sanding.

"You know, I ordered new canvas material to recover these frames, but I think I might send it back. I mean, I can afford to keep it, but why? I think, even though these paintings are fucking ugly, the canvas itself isn't ruined. I'll put a coat of primer over it, and it's..." I chuckled at my own joke, "a blank canvas." I roared so loudly with laughter that I scared Bushy away.

I sanded until they were smooth to the touch, wet a rag with the hose, and I wiped off the canvases to remove the dust. I took off my T-shirt and held the hose over my head to rinse the dust and sweat from my hair, face, and arms before I made a mess inside. I pulled my hair back up and went into the cabin, heading to the bedroom before I froze my ass off.

I changed out of the wet jeans and sneakers into a pair of gray sweats and a black sweatshirt. The sun was lower in the sky and the air was chilling fast.

I went to the dresser and opened the top drawer. Inside were a few remnants from my former life—my credit cards with my real name on them, my driver's license that I never carried, the vintage 30 MM Cartier Ruby Pocket Watch that had been a birthday gift from Alistaire when I turned thirty, and the notebook that had added insult to injury—Alistaire's handwritten diary.

I picked up the diary and carried it to the kitchen, where I opened the fridge and grabbed a beer to take outside with me. The canvases needed to dry before I began priming them, and I needed to purge the pain more than I needed to breathe.

Taking a seat on the top step of the front porch, I stared down the mountain at the small valley town of Foggy Basin. Bushy jumped back up on the porch about three feet away. "As I was saying before you so rudely took off, I miss the smell of turpentine. I used to clean up with it when I was painting, and Alistaire would bitch about it endlessly, which I relished. He did enough shit to piss me off, and it was my passive-aggressive way of getting back at him."

I sipped my beer and put it on the porch next to me. "There came a time in our relationship when we seemed to do everything that we could to piss each other off. I really didn't know why until after Alistaire killed himself and I found this in his things." I held up the diary.

Flipping through it, I found the page that had ruined me. I'd read it so many times I couldn't count. The ink was faded and smeared where my tears had fallen onto it as the words he'd written had cut into my soul.

"After Alistaire drowned himself rather than coming home to me, I had to call his parents to tell them he had died in Chicago. Dumb-ass stole a boat and took it out into a terrible snow and windstorm. Anyway, his parents played the blame game, just as I expected they would. Never liked me, but I'm sure you already guessed that.

"I was boxing up his things because the Scotts had insisted I send them everything that was Alistaire's. They threatened to sue me if I didn't. I fought them until I found this." I stared down at that blurry page that was the first entry before reading it out loud to Bushy.

December 16, 2022

Today is a day I'll never forget. Today, I met the love of my life. This boy is meant to be mine. I'll always remember the big smile on his beautiful face when Dierdre introduced us. "Tariq Jackson, this is Alistaire Scott. He's going to consult on the screen adaptation of his book, Lovers to Enemies. *It's the one Del told you about. Alistaire, this is Tariq Jackson. He's just started filming* Rubber to the Road."

My Tariq nodded. "I've been wanting to meet you, Mr. Scott. The book is phenomenal. The way you wove their love affair into the mystery they needed to solve that ultimately breaks them apart is masterful. Hell, I'd love to sit down and discuss it with you."

I thought I'd faint right there. He's so beautiful and funny and has the potential to be the perfect boy! I can't wait to see him again.

I glanced at Bushy. "Alistaire was a Daddy. He thought I'd be his perfect boy, but we were too much alike. Twice, I agreed to go with him to a club and share a boy when he wanted to play out a fantasy, but I didn't like sharing Alistaire. Apparently, I was an idiot to think I could continue to make him happy after those experiences."

The squirrel made a *muk-muk* sound. "You're a smart woman? Man? Anyway, yes. Tariq Jackson was happy to be the boy who stole Alistaire's heart right before Christmas of 2021."

I flipped a few more pages, skipping everything Alistaire thought Tariq was perfect at doing. Alistaire was thrilled to have Tariq as his boy, and he couldn't wait to get away from me, but he wasn't sure how to do it. The next faded page reminded me of the mistake we'd made that I would always regret. I was never one to share.

> *January 16, 2023*
>
> *Tariq has agreed to be my boy. He asked me to leave Mosby and move in together. He wants us to make a life, and I can't deny him. I've fallen so deeply in love with him that I don't know where I end and he begins. I care for Mosby and always will. We've been together for ten years, and we've had a lot of good times, through thick and thin, as poets say. I've come to realize I love him, but I'm not in love with him. Not the way I am with my boy, Tariq.*
>
> *It feels wrong to stay with Mosby out of obligation, but how do we unwind us? How much will Mosby hate me if I leave?*

"A hell of a lot." I couldn't keep the anger inside any longer. I wasn't a boy, but I didn't hate the idea of having a boy. I simply couldn't see myself ever sharing a significant other in my life. I wasn't built that way.

Bushy scampered into the yard toward the bird feeder, scurrying up the pole and sitting on the perch. "Don't eat the millet. I'll get something better for you."

I put down the diary and went inside, coming back with a paper plate filled with dried fruit and nuts. I put the plate on the porch floor, along with a small bowl of water, and then I sat back down.

"So, Barbara Bushy, dinner and a monologue? Sure, why not." I took another sip of my beer before putting down the bottle and picking up the diary.

I glanced at Bushy, who really had become domesticated since I'd moved into the cabin. "You know, everybody isn't like me. Some folks might shoot and eat you."

Bushy *kuk-kuked* her disapproval at me, which made me laugh. I stood and walked over to the canvases, touching them to feel if they were dry.

While my squirrel friend ate her food, I painted a coat of gesso on the canvases and then walked around the back of the house to grab the copper pot I'd used to have a fire in the fall and winter when the cabin felt as though it was closing in on me.

I put it in the driveway and gathered some firewood to fill it. I went to the shed and grabbed the lighter fluid, returning to soak the wood for an easier light later. It was still warm enough that I didn't need a fire right now, but once the sun set, it would be nice.

After a second coat to the canvases, I went inside and took a shower, pulling on a pair of pajama pants and a T-shirt before shoving my feet into a pair of athletic slides. I grabbed a bag of chips that Tyler had put into the cooler, another beer, and headed outside. I had a couple of plastic chairs on the front porch, so I picked one up and carried it to the yard.

Bushy was still hanging out in a nearby tree, so I lit a match and tossed it onto the fuel-soaked wood.

The fire caught without trouble, and I sat in the plastic chair, turning my eyes to Bushy. "This will be the last time I read this diary, Bushy. I've been hiding and nursing a broken heart for a year. I'm really not sure why it broke. Alistaire and I had lost the love we once had for each other, and he'd moved on. He just hadn't moved out."

> *February 12, 2023*
>
> *Mosby is insisting that he's going to meet me in New York for Valentine's Day. I'll be able to spend the next week with Tariq after he leaves, but I plan to tell Mosby it's over between us when we're in Manhattan.*

> *I'll give him everything. I've got a new book started that I haven't told Mosby about. It's an insta-love gay romance about an actor and a writer who meet by chance and fall madly in love. Yes, it's a bit of a biography, so shoot me! It's set at Christmastime, so I'll finish it over the summer and push for its release at Thanksgiving. In the dedication, I'm planning to ask Tariq to marry me.*

I exhaled. "You hear that, Bushy? The man who never wanted to get married *wanted* to get married. How's that for a slap in the face?"

I stood from the chair and carried my beer and the diary over to the blaze. I looked down the hill to the valley below and wondered if life gave us second chances. Wouldn't it be ironic if my only chance at love killed himself because he loved another man?

I glanced at the diary again. "Alistaire, I hope you and Tariq are together...in hell." I tossed the book into the fire and watched it burn. I never wanted to read those words again. The time for wallowing was done.

Thursday morning, I got up with the sun and went for a run...which I hadn't done for a year at least. When I got back, quite breathless, Bushy was sitting in the plastic chair I'd left in the yard. I had to smile. "Breakfast, milady?"

Wednesday night, I researched how to become a barber, which was an odd thing for me to care about, but it was interesting. Tyler Rockwell was heavy on my mind. I'd had a dream about him and woken up with an aching cock he'd been showing a lot of love to in my dream. It was hard to get back to sleep until I took myself in hand, and even after, I dreamed Tyler was resting his head on my chest as I rubbed the soft skin of his back.

"Okay, Bushy. I'm going to Hartsville to pick up some produce, new paint brushes, and maybe some shingles to fix the roof. I'll be back this afternoon." I put the paper plate on the porch floor and went to shower. An hour later, I was dressed in jeans with no paint yes, I had a pair—and climbing into the truck to make the thirty-mile trek.

I turned on my phone to use the GPS to get to the fresh produce market in town. There was also a farm supply store where I could get some shingles to patch a persistent leak in the shed roof. How I'd fix it was another mystery to be solved.

I'd pulled my hair into a bun after my shower and trimmed my beard to keep from being mistaken for a vagrant, and I'd thought about the little barber in the valley. The temptation was strong to ask him to cut my hair and shape my beard, but I had an alert set for any time my name was in the news, and with the one-year anniversary of Alistaire's suicide having just happened, I'd been mentioned a few times.

I wasn't ready to jump back into the backstabbing world of art. I was enjoying my freedom and didn't want to return to the grind yet.

When I arrived at the produce market, I retrieved the cloth grocery bags from the passenger seat. As I walked through the entrance, the beautiful array of colorful vegetables had my mouth watering.

I was loading some peppers into my grocery sack when I felt a tap on my shoulder. I turned to see a vaguely familiar, beautiful Latina standing behind me with a stunning smile. "You're Leslie, right?"

I was surprised. "Uh, yeah. You're…"

The woman grinned. "I'm Camila Ortiz. I work at Shear Bliss with Tyler."

"Oh, uh, yes. That's where I saw you. How's everything? I hope he conveyed to his mother that I had no plans to sue her." Just my damn luck to run into someone close to the guy I was trying to forget.

"Yes. He explained everything to Marlena, and she was relieved. They're both very special people, and I know they were worried. Maybe send Ty a note that you're fine. Do you have a phone? I can give you Tyler's number."

I reached into my pocket and handed her my cell because she didn't look like someone who would take no for an answer. Camila quickly pecked in something and handed it back to me.

"Ty is a sweet guy. He's had a difficult past. He needs someone who will see what a wonderful man he is and not try to change him. Think about it."

An older woman stepped up and touched Camila's arm, saying something in Spanish, which wasn't my forte. Camila turned and smiled, responding to the woman before taking her basket filled with many different peppers and chilis.

"Can you freeze those and use them later?" I pointed to the basket.

Camila gave me an odd look, but she grinned and repeated my question, I was guessing, in Spanish. The older woman nodded and went into a long explanation. Finally, Camila nodded and turned to me.

"Yes."

I chuckled. "All of those words mean yes?"

Camila giggled. "She went into detail about blanching them for three to five minutes before you cut them, and...just look it up. Abuela does it all the time. Anyway, call Ty."

The two of them chattered lively as they walked away. I went about picking out vegetables and putting them into my cloth bags. I looked up easy recipes on my phone that I could try using the vegetables I'd collected, and I decided it was worth giving it a shot.

After I checked out at the fresh produce market, I got into the truck and rolled down the window. My phone was in the pocket of my jeans, so I fished it out to send a text to Tyler. I didn't want to be on the wrong side of Camila.

> I started the truck and drove to the art supply shop near the lumber yard. After parking in the lot the two stores shared, my phone buzzed. I reached for it on the bench seat next to me and hopped out, seeing a quick response from Tyler.

> **Hi! I didn't know you had a phone, or I'd have asked to share numbers. Are you doing okay?**

Was I ever going to tell him the truth about not being a vagrant? His surprise at the fact I had a phone was a sure sign he still believed I didn't have a pot to piss in.

I went into the art supply store with a silly smile on my face. Something inside me was quite happy Tyler had responded and admired how he hadn't asked prying questions like whether I had enough to eat. I planned to return the Rockwells' kindnesses when I figured out the best way to do so.

> **I'm fine, really. I made it home okay. Barbara Bushy missed me, I think.**

> **Barbara Bushy? Is she married to George H. W. Bushy?**

I chuckled. The joke was obvious, but it was cute coming from him. I could almost picture his bright smile.

> **Barbara Bushy is my pet squirrel. It's a long story, but she—I think it's a she—keeps me company.**

> **That's so cute. I'd like to hear the story sometime. I mean, if you ever come back to Foggy Basin. Was your home okay when you returned?**

Okay, maybe he believed I had a home. That was nice. He definitely had a kind streak I hadn't been exposed to in quite a while. God knew not many people in SoCal had it.

> **Everything was fine. I'm planning to explore my canning options. Camila's grandmother sparked my interest again as she explained about blanching peppers—or so Camila explained because I don't speak Spanish. Anyway, Camila's very fond of you.**

> **She is protective, I guess you could say. Did she threaten you? I'll talk to her if she did. You don't deserve that.**

As I knew, he was a kind and lovely soul. The more we chatted, the more the pull was for me to return to Foggy Basin.

> **I don't suppose you know anything about patching a roof?**

> **What do you think? LOL! But I might know someone who can offer advice. Do you want me to have him call you?**

Of course, he was nice enough to offer to have someone help me fix the roof. How could I say no?

> **If you think he knows what he's doing, then please. I'll pay him. I'm not a craftsman with those types of jobs.**

> **I'll check with them and get back to you. Can we keep chatting? Where do you live?**

I shoved my phone in my pocket and went to finish my shopping. I couldn't decide if it was smart to continue to chat with him or better to leave things alone?

Something inside me said to keep going but not to give up where I lived yet. I wasn't sure why, but I knew I wasn't ready for anything more with the beautiful man. I needed more time to figure myself out.

Chapter Seven
Tyler

Friday morning, I awoke at seven to have my video call with my therapist, who was on the East Coast. Thankfully, it went better than I had expected.

As I leafed through the journal I'd been keeping at the doctor's request, I found the picture Leslie had drawn of me, which was remarkably good, in my uneducated opinion. It made me smile. After I finished the call, I tore it out of my notebook and put it on the front of the fridge with a magnet.

I was early for work and a little on edge. I'd been waiting for another text from Leslie on Wednesday evening and all day Thursday, but I'd gotten nothing. I didn't want to contact him without receiving a response because I was sure it would make me come across as clingy, so I chewed my nails and kept my phone in my pocket to know immediately if he responded.

"Ty, can you shampoo Bonnie?" I glanced over to where Mom stood at her station, finishing the cut for Teresa Schmidt. Her next client, Bonnie Jordan, sat in the waiting area, flipping through an old gossip rag.

I longed for the day when I had too many clients to be the fallback to shampoo everyone else's or sweep up the hair others cut. I had skills. I just needed to be able to show them what I knew.

"Sure, Mom." I walked out to the front to grab Bonnie Jordan. "Hi, Mrs. Jordan. If you'll follow me back, I'll shampoo you."

Bonnie was a nice, widowed woman who'd returned to Foggy Basin after her husband died in San Francisco. She now lived with her elderly mother. She worked at the post office part-time and was very active in the community. She coordinated the library fundraiser every March and was on the committee that planned Foggy Basin Days in the fall.

The town council selected a different community project every year to use the proceeds from the Foggy Basin Ball and Bake Sale. The previous year before I got out of Folsom, they put a new roof on the library and repaved the parking lot behind it. Mom said it was quite an improvement.

Bonnie sat in the shampoo chair, and I adjusted the back for her. She was about five-two and thin. She needed a little support, so I grabbed a pillow from the couch in the waiting area and slid it under her lower back to keep her high enough so her head was in the bowl. "How's that?"

"It's better, Tyler. How've you been?" Bonnie wasn't like some of the others who frequented the shop. I liked her. She wasn't judgmental at all.

"I've been good. Getting used to being back home. How's Ivy? She went to college in New York, right?"

Bonnie had lost her husband when Ivy was in middle school, and when they'd moved back to town, Ivy had been in my grade. She was one of the nice girls who didn't give me shit. We weren't friends, but I didn't hate Ivy.

"She went to SUNY-Courtland, Tyler. Ivy's now teaching school in Oregon. She's got a boyfriend who teaches at the same school, and I'm going to visit them next week." Bonnie smiled happily, which was nice to see.

"That's so great to hear, Mrs. Jordan. Tell her I said hi. When will Foggy Basin Days take place this year? What's the project?" Bonnie giggled as I gently shampooed her hair.

"This year, it will be the second weekend in September. We're collecting money for a new playground at Veterans Park. Do you cook, Tyler? We're looking for people to donate baked goods for the baked-goods raffle."

I rinsed her hair and brushed it with a deep conditioner. Bonnie's hair was starting to gray, and was a little dry. I was sure Mom would set her up with a good hair-care routine when she left, but right now, I'd do what I knew Mom would—condition the hell out of it.

"I'm not a baker. I can make a ham and cheese sandwich, but that's about as far as my culinary talents can take me."

Bonnie laughed out loud. "Your baking can't be any worse than some of the others in town. The prune with walnuts cake was the one thing we couldn't get rid of last year."

It was my turn to laugh. "Prune and walnuts cake? That doesn't even sound good. You should talk to Mom about her bacon-cheese-jalapeño cornbread. She does it in an iron skillet, and it's so good. She makes amazing—"

"Honey butter. Yes, I've won the basket with it for the last four years. My mother loves it, so it's my job to bid the most. It's one of those things I don't want us to have too often because it would be less special, but I'm already looking forward to it this fall."

I grinned as I wrapped her hair in a warm towel. "You want some cucumber water or maybe sparkling water with lemon?"

"I'd love some cucumber water, Tyler. Thank you."

I left her with her eyes closed and went to the kitchen to get Bonnie a drink. When I returned, I saw Mom finishing up with Teresa Schmidt, the grade school principal.

"Here you go, Ms. Jordan. I'll rinse you in about five minutes, and Mom will be ready for you." Bonnie nodded, and I stepped away to grab the broom and clean up Mom's station while she was upfront chatting with Ms. Schmidt.

As I was sweeping up around Mom's chair, my phone chimed in the pocket of my apron. I stopped sweeping and pulled it from the pocket. There was a message from Leslie.

> **I left your cooler on the back porch of your apartment. Thank you for the food. I appreciated it. I hope you had a good week. Leslie.**

I hurried out the back door of the salon and ran into the alley, looking up at the small porch by my apartment entrance. The small blue cooler was at the top with a bow on the handle, which made me grin. I couldn't wait for the day to be over so I could see if there was anything inside.

But before that happened, I had my first client coming in. German Belmonte was due in my chair at three-forty-five, and I was excited...and a little nervous.

"Tyler, your new client is here." I was busy stocking my station with combs, shaving soap, and towels when Alice came over wearing a huge smile.

I took a breath and followed her to the front, seeing German standing at the desk looking very anxious. Ramon was sitting on a couch with a sweet smile aimed at German, and it touched my heart.

"German, glad to see you. Let's go back and talk about what you'd like to have done." I turned to Ramon. "Come on back with us."

We walked to my station, and I welcomed German into my chair. "Ramon, Edina is gone for the day, so please sit." I put my hand on the back of Edina's chair and turned it toward mine. "Can I get you guys something to drink? We have soda, juice, coffee, and water."

German glanced at Ramon, who laughed. "He's nervous and stubborn. We're okay right now. Ger, babe, tell Tyler what you want."

I turned the chair to face the mirror and smiled. "Is it okay if I run my fingers through your hair? I'd like to get an idea of the thickness and your scalp health."

"His hair is thick and gorgeous, and I love wrapping my hands in it. I'll miss it." Ramon smirked.

German rolled his eyes. "Ignore my husband. Yes, please tell me what I need. I don't think I want to cut off too much."

I was a little stunned by German's acknowledgment that he and Ramon were married, but...

"Whoa! Are you fucking kidding me?"

There was a lot of Spanish after that because it seemed as if Camila didn't know her brother had gotten married either.

Ramon responded to her fervently, and as I looked in the mirror, I could see the smirk on German's face. Camila dragged her brother outside, and I turned my attention back to my new client.

"So, uh, congratulations? Let's talk about your hair. What do you want, German?"

"Shoulder-length so I can still put it up when I cook. Look, my hair's been this long since I was young, but I'm going to be thirty in a few weeks. We just got married—" we both heard Camila's shrieking through the back door "—and I'm going to meet Ramon's extended family tomorrow. Can you make me look presentable?"

I smirked. "As if you need me for that. When did you guys get married?"

"Last weekend. We drove to Vegas and got married in one of those cheesy wedding chapels. I didn't hate it."

I combed German's gorgeous hair and folded a large chunk of it up, sweeping it over his shoulder. "That's about six inches. Is that too short?"

Much to my surprise, German laughed. "Not if you know what to do with it." Then, we both laughed at his innuendo.

I smacked him on the shoulder. "Is this too short? Are you going to cry if I cut off too much? I can start with about half of that if you want to check it."

German laughed. "Naw. Go for it."

"You know, you have beautiful hair. If you'd consider going up four more inches, we could donate your hair to Beautiful Lengths. Mom has a friend who coordinates it in San Fran, so we'd section your hair into three braids and cut off ten inches. It would still be long enough to pull it back while you cook. It's just a suggestion."

Ramon and Camila finally returned inside, and Ramon returned to Edina's station. I spun German's chair and doubled up the hair, holding it up in his direction. "Your husband could donate this much hair to a charity that makes wigs for individuals with cancer. What do you think? He'd still be able to pull it back when he cooks." I pulled the hair back and showed Ramon how it might look.

Ramon stood and walked over to his husband. "What do you want to do, *mi amor*? Whatever makes you happy."

My heart skipped a beat at hearing the love in their voices as they spoke in hushed tones. Finally, Ramon gave German a quick kiss on the cheek and sat down. I turned German's chair and caught his reflection in the mirror as he smiled. "Go ahead and do it. I like the idea of donating it."

I didn't want the guy to freak out. He had about a foot on me, and he was crazy muscular. "Are you sure?"

German turned to Ramon. "Come over here and cut the first chunk."

Ramon smirked and stepped forward. I quickly sectioned off the hair and put a rubber band around the first section, braiding it and putting another band at the bottom.

"Here you go." I handed Ramon my scissors and stepped back a little.

Ramon held up the section and the scissors. "You're sure about this?"

German reached back and squeezed Ramon's thigh, nodding a bit. Ramon made the first cut, handing the braid to me.

"Thank you, German, Ramon. This will be used to help someone who's lost their hair." I then went about braiding the rest of German's hair and doing the same thing Ramon had done. When I cut the last braid, the stylists in the salon were standing behind us clapping, and Camila took a picture of the three of us each holding one of the braids. It was a beautiful moment.

"You did a fantastic job, Ty," Mom told me as I swept up the salon. German had left with a happy smile, and Ramon was running his fingers through German's shorter hair, pulling it and laughing. They were cute. I was glad they were happy.

Mom had put the braids into a plastic bag and then shoved it into a mailing envelope. She addressed it as I pushed the loose hair I'd swept into the hair vac behind the reception desk.

"Thanks, Mom. He had beautiful hair, and it was easy to shape it for him after I cut off the length. What are you doing tonight?"

Mom pretended to be busy at the computer, but I knew there was nothing she needed to do. I'd taken care of everything while I waited for German all day.

"I, uh, I thought I'd balance the books." *Okay, that's a lie.*

"Did you not check the desk in the back? I did that yesterday. I can run the tax forms on Monday when the final bank statements are received. Where are you *really* going?"

Mom stared at me for a moment before she sighed. "Tyler, honey, I'd rather not talk about it right now, if you don't mind. I ran into an old friend. We lost touch a long time ago, but he's very nice, okay? We're going out for coffee."

I was happy for her, but I was still going to rake her over the coals. "Who is it? Is it someone I know? Where are you going? You're not going to drink and drive, are you? You know I can't come get you."

I was rattling off the questions the same way Mom used to do when I was younger. I was still so damn grateful she'd been the mother she had, but I owed her the interrogation for all the times she'd quizzed me. If she hadn't been the Marlena Rockwell who raised me with love, I probably would have been dead after the way I fucked up.

"I... Tyler, I don't owe you any explanations." Mom's hands flew to her hips in a stance I'd seen too many times as I was growing up.

I laughed. "No ma'am, you don't. I'm just hassling you the way you used to hassle me."

I walked over to her and pulled her into my arms. "I love you. I want you to make sure the guy is worthy of you. You deserve only the best." I kissed her cheek and pulled away.

Mom popped me on the chest, but I noticed her covertly wiping her eyes. "I love you too, Ty. Lock up after me. Have a good night."

I followed Mom to the front door and walked her outside to her little SUV. I hugged her again and kissed her cheek before I went back inside and cleaned up for the evening. I locked the front door and hurried to get ready for the half-day on Saturday.

After everything was ready for the morning, I turned off the lights and closed the back door. I locked it and hurried upstairs to my apartment. There, by the door, was the cooler I'd given Leslie.

I picked it up, and it was heavier than I'd expected. Once inside, I carried it through to the small kitchen area and opened it. Inside were four jars and a handwritten note.

> *Tyler—*
>
> *Thank you for the food. Here are a few jars of things that I made. They'll last for months because they've been properly canned, according to YouTube directions. The green jar is a poblano and tomatillo salsa, and the red one is a tomato and red chili corn salsa. The other two are marinara. Maybe we can find recipes to make together? Give me a call if you want company.*
>
> *Leslie*
>
> *820-555-6392 (in case you deleted my number since you haven't texted lately)*

My mood lightened exponentially. I quickly pulled my phone from my pocket and shot off a text.

> **Thank you for the homemade canned goods. I'd love to research recipes with you. As you know, my kitchen is small, but I could ask to use Mom's kitchen. Let me know.**

I hoped he responded. I doubted I'd get a good night's sleep until he did.

Chapter Eight
Mosby

I should have stuck around after dropping off the cooler, but I was still trying to figure out how I felt about the dreams induced by Tyler's handsome face. When I placed the cooler onto his back porch and walked toward my truck, I glanced into the salon to see Tyler cutting the hair of a handsome guy. I was immediately jealous, which was stupid. I barely knew Tyler and had no claim to him.

After I carried the last jars to the root cellar and stacked them on a shelf I'd made, I walked upstairs to the porch and sat in the chair I used when I painted. I wished I could see how Tyler reacted when he saw the cooler, but then again, did I care? Why would I? It was merely a repayment of his kindness for giving me food. *Riiiight...*

Barbara Bushy ran into the yard from the large oak tree and sat at the bottom of the stairs. "Good afternoon, Ms. Bushy. I left your plate over there?"

Barbara scampered up the stairs and over to the paper plate and the water bowl. She sat on her haunches and picked up a piece of banana to nibble before turning to stare at me.

"So, you like bananas? Good to know. Now, what do I do about young Tyler? He is quite handsome, and I can't stop thinking about him? What would you suggest I do?"

Barbara Bushy glared at me. I was guessing she thought I was an idiot. "Oh, you think I'm stupid?"

Of course, she didn't say it out loud, but the look she gave me? I could see her intent. While I respected Barbara Bushy for her companionship, I was a bit peeved at her judgment.

"Hey, you don't know how I suffered after I lost Alistaire because I haven't told you about every minute that we were together. I loved him."

Barbara Bushy chattered for a moment and then trained her eyes on me again, not blinking.

"Okay, maybe *loved* was a bit strong, but we were supposed to be partners. We pledged to make a life together."

The squirrel chattered again, but I didn't speak squirrel. I could only infer what she was getting at, and I was a little pissed. "Look, yes, Alistaire and I hadn't been as close as we were when we began our relationship, but it didn't help that he cheated on me. Hell, I know he cheated multiple times, and I'm sure there are many more I didn't know about.

"Bottom line is that I have a hard time trusting anyone after what happened with Alistaire falling in love with Tariq Jackson. *I never cheated!*"

Yes, I was shouting, but dammit, I had done nothing wrong. Barbara stared at me, and I could imagine her asking why I was keeping Tyler at arm's length.

"I don't know!"

Suddenly, everything was quiet as I watched Barbara scurry from the porch. The idea that she'd called me on why I was keeping Tyler at bay didn't sit well with me. I barely knew the kid. I wasn't ready to consider what was next for me, and now a squirrel was telling me what to do? That was fucking ridiculous.

I jolted awake, trying to figure out what the hell had just happened. "Did you really dream about having an argument with a fucking squirrel?"

I sat up and looked out the window to see the sun was coming up. I had to ask myself what the hell that dream was about. The inner turmoil made my gut ache, but I'd learned one lesson. I needed to see the handsome barber again. I was attracted to him, and fighting it made me absolutely squirrely.

With my agent still hunting for me, I was hesitant to go to Foggy Basin. I was sure she had spies everywhere, and I didn't want to chance that I'd be spotted and my solitude would come to an end.

Early on, I'd dumped my old cell and phone number, and I'd bought a new one through a shell company I'd created to consolidate my assets when I first decided to get away from it all. I wanted the conveniences I'd had in my old life without being found, and Moslie Consolidated, LLC provided the privacy I sought.

I wasn't ready to jump back into the art world. It was a ruthless clusterfuck, and I'd been fed up with all of it when my world imploded. However, one fact remained: I missed painting something with meaning. The landscapes I had been painting could be sold at a box store for a buck.

After I went through my morning routine, I went outside with my coffee and sat on the front porch step, scanning the yard to see if Barbara Bushy had returned. The morning was warm and sunny, though the trees offered a nice bit of shade that I wanted to capture in a painting...with Tyler Rockwell in the foreground.

I'd already drawn one sketch of him the night I'd slept at his apartment. He starred in my dreams every night—except for the previous night when Barbara Bushy took center stage—and I needed to get some of those scenes on paper so I could get a good night's sleep.

I went back inside and grabbed a sketch pad off the table by the front door, along with a few pencils. I refilled my coffee mug and headed back outside. Barbara Bushy was nibbling on some acorns she'd gathered from under the oak tree. "I'm barely holding on by a thread, Barbara. Don't start any shit with me today." She turned her back and continued to eat. Apparently, I was filled with residual anger from my dream, and she was having none of it.

I closed my eyes for a moment and focused. Tyler's stunning brown eyes came to me first with the little glints of gold that reflected the sun. I had noticed them when he helped me up from the sidewalk in front of Shear Bliss.

I began sketching, his handsome face filling my mind's eye. His pouty mouth was calling to me, and I wished like hell I'd kissed him when I had the chance. He was slender with compact muscles and an ass that looked like two puppies fighting under a blanket. It would take me a million squats to achieve that amount of definition.

Unless I drew his head on backward, I couldn't highlight his ass, so I only drew him from the waist up and then I concentrated on the background. The glint of sunshine off the car windows parked in front of the businesses along Main Street added a bit of movement.

There were signs in front of the dozen or so stores, shops, and eateries. Flags hung from the light poles, bragging about Foggy Basin being a historic shopping district. Their bright purple colors waving in the breeze stood out from the green and brown hues of the trees lining the streets.

The only store I'd found on Main Street that I liked was Beauty and the Boutique. It was definitely not farmer-chic like many of the stores I'd seen in neighboring towns. Ezra had a sense of style that was all his own, and his boutique reminded me of the haute couture I'd seen in shops on Rodeo Drive.

I took the sketch inside to my studio, dragging two easels over to the window—one for the sketch pad and one for a canvas. After opening the supply closet, I gathered a plastic palette and the colors I needed from the rows of paints.

My brushes were already in a large coffee can, heads up so they'd dry properly, and I grabbed a few rags from the bag I'd ordered.

Once I had everything where I wanted it, I sat and stared at the too-white canvas for thirty minutes, suddenly forgetting everything I'd just played in my head. "I need to see him again."

I went to shower and dress, pulling my hair back in a bun before I hopped into the old Bronco and drove to Foggy Basin. I had no reason to go, and no clue what I'd say to Tyler when I got there, but something inside me pulled me toward the town.

Thirty-minutes later, I parked on the lot across from the grocery store. I stopped on the sidewalk and stared across the street, seeing Tyler laughing and chatting with the customers through the salon window. His smile was infectious.

I strolled down the street, his handsome face on my mind, and wandered into Don't Go Bakin' my Heart, the local bakery on Main Street. The baker, a man named Percy, was restocking some fancy pastries and was humming along with the satellite radio station that was playing French music. It was sort of odd, but then again, what else were you going to do when you were trapped in a small bakery starting at god-knew-how early? You'd learn the playlist and hum along.

I perused the cases and found some fruit tarts and croissants, so I ordered a dozen of each. "Special occasion?" Percy seemed nervous. Was it because he was alone in the bakery with me? Did I already have a reputation as a jackass? Most people in that town were annoyingly friendly.

"Just a thank-you present for some nice people."

Percy packaged my things beautifully, and after I paid, he gave me a nervous smile. "I hope they enjoy them. I made them today. Have a great day."

"Thank you."

I paid, grabbed the bag with the goods, and left. When I approached the stairs to Shear Bliss, I saw that the bottom step was freshly repaired, which made me smile. There was yellow caution tape around half of the step, which led me to believe it had been done earlier that morning.

Stepping closer to the repair, I saw the concrete was still wet. I fought the temptation to swipe my initials into it. Instead, I put a little heart there to commemorate my entrance into Tyler's life. It was something only I'd know the significance of, but going forward when I walked by that step, I'd remember the beautiful man.

The little bell over the door rang as I walked inside. A young woman I didn't recognize stood behind the desk where I'd seen Tyler standing the day I fell. "Welcome to Shear Bliss. How can I help you?"

She was cute and pleasant—too pleasant—but I couldn't fault her for it. "Is Tyler Rockwell here?"

"Oh! Do you have an appointment with Tyler?"

I exhaled. "No, I don't. I was the lame-ass guy who tripped over the step. I wanted to thank Tyler and Miss Marlena for taking care of me. Are either of them available?"

"I'm Alice, by the way. Give me a second." She hurried away, and I was beginning to feel like a damn fool. I shouldn't have come. I damn well shouldn't have brought sweets.

I glanced around to see nobody nearby staring at me. I dropped the box on the desk and headed toward the door. Just before I walked out, I felt a gentle hand on my bicep.

I turned to see a beautiful, smiling face. "Hi, Leslie. How've you been?" Tyler pointed at the box on the counter. "I've wondered how you're doing. What's that?"

"Just a thank-you gift for you and your coworkers. I'm sorry if I was a pain in the ass. I appreciate what you did for me." I stared into those beautiful brown eyes and did my best to memorize them.

"Thank you very much. Are you okay? Any lasting issues from your almost concussion?"

"Not really. Just a short lapse in memories. It's all cleared up now. Have dinner with me at Midnight Pleasure? Or if you're game, I found a couple of recipes we can try out." Where the fuck did that come from? I had no recipes to try.

"I'd love to have dinner with you." There was that killer smile. It would be the death of me. How the fuck could I get out of it?

"Where would you like to cook? My kitchen's not a chef's dream, but my mom will be gone. I'll ask if we can use her kitchen."

His mother's place? Hell no. "Uh, how about my place? I'll come back for you. I'll shop while you finish up here."

I must have lost my fucking mind. I came to town to get another look at him, and here I was, inviting him into my safe space, my sanctuary. Who the fuck had control of my big damn mouth, because, surely it wasn't me.

"I hate that you have to come back to town or stick around to wait for me." *Yeah, I hate it too. Tell them you need to leave right now.*

"It's fine. What time do you get off? From work, I mean?"

Tyler chuckled at my unintended double entendre. "Five. We're closing at five today."

I nodded. "Okay then, I'll be back at five." We smiled at each other, and I left before I committed to something more outrageous. How the fuck would I kill a whole day in this one-horse town?

Chapter Nine
Tyler

Mom had another date that afternoon with the guy she wouldn't discuss, regardless of how well I hid the question in a comment. "Where are you eating dinner with your date?" "Yeah, I couldn't imagine dating a guy who was a street sweeper. What's your date do, Mom?"

She would laugh at me and walk away, refusing to tell me anything about her man, so I finally gave up prying. I wasn't sure I wanted to know much about some guy who might be banging my mother. The thought completely skeeved me out.

"He's a nice guy, and for right now, that's all you need to know." I rolled my eyes and kissed her cheek.

"Fine. You look gorgeous. I hope he deserves all this beauty." I prayed like hell the guy was indeed nice because my mother deserved nothing but the best.

I hurried to clean the salon as much as I could before everyone was finished for the day. Alice would be closing the shop because she had a client coming at six for a balayage color, so she'd be there for hours. I planned to check on the salon before I went to bed that night, but I was confident everything would be fine.

At five on the dot, there was a knock on my apartment door. I tried to calm down because this wasn't a date. Or was it? No, no. If it was a date, Leslie would have said so. We were just going to cook together.

I opened the door and smiled, seeing Leslie with a grin as well. "Come in. You look quite handsome." Stepping aside, Leslie walked into my apartment and turned around. His hair was still in a bun from earlier, but he wasn't wearing his leather jacket. He was drool worthy.

"You're looking quite handsome yourself. You ready to go to the store? I had a few errands to run today in Hartsville, so I didn't shop yet. I parked my Bronco on the street in front of the salon, so if I don't want to get a ticket for going over the allotted one-hour parking limit, we should get going."

I grabbed my jacket and slid my arms inside before picking up my house keys and wallet from the table nearby. I followed him outside, locking my door before we went down the stairs. "So, you have a vehicle? Where was it while you were recuperating at my place?" The embarrassment from assuming he was unhoused and living in the woods was still fresh.

"It belonged to my grandfather. He left it to me, along with the family cabin and the land. The Bronco's been refurbished—more recently by the mechanic at Twisted Chassis—several times over the years. That day, I had parked it in the public parking lot across the street. I'd gone shopping at the grocery store before I fell, but I accidentally left my wallet in the truck. I was on my way to get it when I tripped over your step."

"Yeah, uh, Mom had it fixed. Again, I'm really sorry—"

Leslie held his finger up and placed it over my lips. "Nope. No more apologies. Let's shop."

We went through the grocery store at a whirlwind pace, and when we got to the checkout, Mr. Willis stared at the two of us. "Can you pay for it this time? It took an hour to put all that produce away."

I glanced at Leslie, who was stunned by the man's rudeness, and I got pissed. "Don't talk to him like that, Mr. Willis. He went to get his wallet and fell over one of the steps in front of the salon. It wasn't his fault he was injured. There's no need for you to be impolite."

George Willis owned the grocery store and could be a real bastard. I still felt bad for Leslie, and I wouldn't dare let George talk to him like that.

Leslie smirked and opened his wallet, handing Mr. Willis a one-hundred-dollar bill. "Got change?" We had only bought thirty dollars' worth of groceries, but it was late, so I was sure Mr. Willis had enough change.

The man held the bill up to the light and stared at it for a moment before he handed it back. "I don't have enough change to break the bill."

"Mr. Willis! That's a downright lie. I've seen people coming and going all day. You can make change." I was appalled by his lack of respect. Leslie hadn't done anything to him.

I reached for my wallet and handed Mr. Willis the exact change, shaking my head as I stared at him. I jerked the hundred from his hand and returned it to Leslie, who hadn't said anything.

Once the groceries were bagged, I jerked the bag out of the old man's hand and pulled Leslie behind me from the store. "I'm so sorry for how he acted. Dinner is on me. That old man owns the only grocery store in this town, and he thinks he can treat people however he wants. That's ridiculous."

We got into his Bronco—which was really old but I could tell he took good care of it—and Leslie started the vehicle. He watched me with a soft smile I didn't understand.

I felt compelled to say something. "What a cool truck. Your grandfather took great care of it." There was an old-school lap belt, so I buckled it. The seats were tan leather and well-worn, but I didn't see any tears in the upholstery. A little pine tree air freshener hung from the rearview mirror, and the scent of pine permeated the inside. It was truly a classic.

"I've run into people like Willis all my life. They like to judge people without knowing one thing about them, which is total bullshit."

My cheeks warmed instantly. "Again, I'm really sorry, Leslie. I suppose I'm as guilty of making wrong assumptions as Mr. Willis."

Wow. Things were off to a rocky start. I reached for the handle to get out when Leslie's arm shot out over my body and locked the door. "I didn't mean you. We'll talk about things when we get to my place."

That was the end of any talking as we drove out of town. Leslie made a left at the stop sign on Main Street, and then a quick right up Mountain View Road. Everyone in Foggy Basin knew what was on Mountain View Road—Lover's Butte.

It was the make-out spot that every kid—probably generations of every kid—knew about. There were also trailheads for hiking. Mom and I used to go up there and hike when I was a kid. When I started driving, I'd go up there by myself, but now, we were all too busy—and it was more of a walk than I wanted to make since I didn't have a license or a car.

"I used to come up here with my mom when I was a kid. There are a lot of really great hiking trails."

I glanced at Leslie. "Is that all you used to do up here?" His face bloomed into an ear-to-ear grin, so obviously, he knew why the place was famous.

I laughed. "Not me, but a lot of the kids I knew came up here. All the guys in my high school were either jocks or jerks, and any gay or bi guys were so deeply in the closet, I don't think they could have found their way out with a map and a flashlight."

That brought a laugh from Leslie, and I liked hearing it. His face appeared a lot younger when he laughed.

"I heard stories about Lover's Butte from my granddad. I guess he may have spent a little time there, back in the day. He grew up in Foggy Basin. He moved to San Francisco for college, where he met Nana. They stayed in the Bay area for my granddad's job and to start their family, but they kept the cabin. It's been in the family for generations."

That was a surprise. I didn't know there was a legacy owner in Foggy Basin. But then again, I hadn't cared about shit like that as a kid, and for the last five years of my life I'd been busy staying alive and out of trouble.

"What's got you hiding out here on the mountain? I know you weren't here when I was in high school. I'd have seen you around town, I'm guessing. I spent a lot of time at Shear Bliss, what with Mom being a single parent." Leslie squirmed a little, his face showing discomfort. "I'm sorry. I'm being nosy. This town does it to you." I put my hand over my mouth to keep from asking more questions.

"No, it's okay. You were honest with me about your time in prison, which I appreciated. Something like that couldn't have been easy for you." His phone pinged on the bench seat between us. He glanced down, turned it screen side down, and sighed.

I almost asked if it was important, but my brain reminded me it wasn't my business. I glanced out the side window at the beautiful trees and wildflowers as we ascended the tall hill.

We drove for about ten minutes without a word being said. I was a little uncomfortable because silence always did that to me. With my mother, there was rarely ever silence unless she was angry. Then she got scary quiet, which was never a good sign. In prison, silence was deadly.

"This is an ironic question, but did you make any friends while in prison? I'm asking because if an ex-boyfriend shows up to claim you, I want to know what to write on my tombstone when he kills me."

I chuckled. "Being seventeen and charged with being an accessory to armed robbery, I was sent to Folsom. I finished high school there, and then my attorney petitioned the court to admit me to a vocational training program in Soledad, which wasn't bad. I was there for eighteen months while I learned to be a barber, and then I was sent back to Folsom, but working as a barber there got me a little better deal. I was housed in a non-affiliated gang unit. I was never in a gang, but there were a lot of former gang members there who would have been killed if they were in GenPop. I worked every day in the barbershop and then had a private cell at night. Mr. Harold was my mentor, but he died right before I got out."

I didn't want to talk about my first two years in Folsom. I'd had it better than some. I wasn't passed around. I roomed with a man who was straight and only wanted blow jobs on occasion because "I ain't no fag, but a man has needs." I mostly took care of him as his wife would have if he hadn't killed her for cheating. Kenny Cook, or KC as he preferred, was never getting out of prison.

"Did you get lonely?" Leslie glanced at me for an instant before he slowed the Bronco to navigate a narrow curve.

"Uh, sometimes. Mostly, I worked with Mr. Harold. He was seventy and had been the barber at Folsom for forty-nine years. He died seven months ago, right before I got released. He was a really nice man."

Harold Rice was in Folsom for going on a robbery spree when he was in his early twenties. He accidentally shot a bank guard that kept him from ever getting parole. Just before I was paroled, he found out he had lung cancer. His lawyer filed a motion for a hardship release, but Mr. Harold died before the parole board took up his case.

"Oh, uh, I'm sorry." Leslie placed his right hand over mine. It was a kind gesture.

"I never knew my dad. Hell, Mom didn't know him very well from what she's told me. Her parents got mad at her when she got pregnant with me, so I never had anyone but Mom. Mr. Harold was like a grandfather to me."

I hadn't talked about him with anyone—not even Mom. His friendship was something just for me. Someone of my very own, and I liked keeping his memory to myself. Why I'd told Leslie was a mystery.

"Um, thanks, Leslie. I miss his advice." *Like what to do about my stupid attraction to you.*

"Ah, we're here." He turned right onto a gravel road. He hopped out and opened the gate, hopping back inside to drive the Bronco through. He then hopped out again and went to the mailbox outside the gate before he closed it and fastened the chain.

He got back behind the wheel, shoved his mail on the dashboard, and drove forward. "You live in a gated community?" I meant it as a corny joke, but Leslie didn't laugh.

"Yeah. Well, I am a gated community. There are people looking for me, and they don't know I'm hiding out here."

My eyes must have doubled in size. "Like from the mob?" I had watched far too much television.

Leslie laughed. "Nothing quite so dangerous, though I'm sure Natalie would like to shoot me if she found me."

Who's Natalie? Please don't have a wife or vindictive girlfriend!

"Is she your former—"

"Agent. Publicist. Lawyer. Name it."

I released a sigh of relief. No wife or girlfriend.

Chapter Ten
Mosby

It was time I came clean with Tyler. I really liked the kid. If my math was right when he'd told me his history, he was twenty-three, and I had turned thirty-nine at the end of February, two days before the anniversary of Alistaire's death. I didn't celebrate anymore. Too many horrible memories associated with it.

Tariq Jackson was twenty-eight when he was with Alistaire, who was forty. Was I falling for the younger man because a younger man had taken Alistaire away from me?

No, that was ridiculous. I was only falling for Tyler because he was a bright light in a dim world.

"Let me print the recipe so we can get started and don't have to rely on my phone. Is it too chilly in here? Should I build a fire in the living room?"

Tyler removed his jacket and shoved his sweater sleeves up to his elbows. "Feels good to me. When we turn on the oven, it'll get warmer." I stepped closer to him, his body inches from mine. I reached around him and took two aprons from the hook. One had been Nana's and the other Granddad's.

"Good point." I put the navy apron over my shoulder and the loop for the white and green apron over Tyler's head. It was shorter.

"Spin around." He did as I instructed, and I quickly tied a bow in the back, taking a moment to look at his sexy bubble butt in a pair of black skinny jeans. It was completely bitable, and the urge was nearly overwhelming.

I stepped back and pulled on my own apron before I took off my loafers and put them on the rug by the back door. Tyler did the same without me saying a word. He followed my lead quite well, sending a flutter through my belly.

"When did you stop wearing makeup?" Tyler definitely didn't need it, but he'd said he enjoyed wearing makeup and nail polish when he was younger. I'd noticed I hadn't seen him wearing either the few times we'd been together.

His cheeks flushed, which was erection-inducing. "I stopped when I went to prison. I was trying to make myself as inconspicuous as possible. There were femme guys there, and they were nice, but they, uh, got passed around. I didn't want that to happen to me."

I touched his shoulder. "Tell me it didn't." I moved my hand to his chin, lifting his face to search his eyes. *Please don't lie to me.*

"I wasn't passed around like the others, but I did have a cell mate who'd offered to look out for me if I took care of him. Do his laundry. Get his food. Carry messages to other inmates when KC was doing a deal. He kept me safe because nobody would cross him."

I glanced down to see Tyler playing with his fingers as if he was nervous. "What else did you have to do for him?"

Tyler swallowed, his Adam's apple bobbing. "He was straight, you see, but he would ask me to blow him sometimes. He said he wasn't gay, so he never wanted to have intercourse with me."

I nodded. "Did you have a choice whether you wanted to or not?"

He shook his head, his eyes falling to the floor in shame. I leaned forward and kissed his forehead before I pulled him into my arms where he began to sniffle. I held him tight. "Never again. I'm so sorry that happened to you. I won't let anything like that happen to you again. How long?"

I reached into the back pocket of my jeans and handed him a handkerchief. He wiped his nose, eyes, and cleared his throat. "I'll wash this and get it back to you. I'm sorry I melted down. I try not to think about it. I was transferred to Soledad, a minimum-security prison, so I could attend trade school there, and while I was gone, KC killed another inmate and was transferred to Pelican Bay supermax in Crescent City. I haven't heard from him, and I don't think he'll ever get out."

That was a relief, actually. That was one worry Tyler wouldn't have.

"Have you, uh, ever been with a guy?" I shouldn't have asked, but I had to know.

Before I walked further out on that limb, I wanted to know if he could be satisfied with one man or if he was like men I'd met over the years who needed variety. Like Alistaire, who believed monogamy to be a heteronormative behavior pushed onto us by the conservatives to fit into the box they'd created when they granted us the freedom to marry. The same heteronormative behavior he was planning to pursue with Tariq.

"I, uh, I've never been fucked by a guy. I've put my fingers inside myself when I masturbate, but no. Not sex with anyone."

"You've never had a boyfriend?" Staring at this beautiful man, I found it hard to believe.

"No. Never had a boyfriend."

My heart pounded in my chest. "Passionately kissed?" He shook his head.

My brain had fireworks going off inside like the Fourth of July. Was Tyler Rockwell my prize for being shit on by Alistaire? "Are you interested in any of those things?"

Tyler swallowed again. "With you?"

I lifted my hand and placed it on the side of his neck, my thumb caressing his Adam's apple.

"Y-yes. Yes, I'd be interested in all those things if I could do them with you." He swallowed again, and the sensation shot through my thumb and up my arm. I leaned closer, brushing my lips over his plump ones. The heat from his body seeped into mine. It was like a warm cup of tea on a cold night.

I didn't deepen it, though god knew I wanted to more than anything, but I needed to tell him my secrets because he trusted me with his.

I pulled away and slowly opened my eyes to see his still closed. I kissed each lid and then his forehead. "We'll never eat if we don't cook." I stepped back and went to a cabinet, retrieving a pasta pot and an iron skillet.

"Leslie?" I put both on the island and turned to Tyler, seeing him playing with his fingers again.

I held up my hand. "The first thing I have to tell you is that my name isn't Leslie. Well, that's not exactly true. Leslie is my last name." I filled the pasta pot with water and turned on the stove.

"Your last name?" The worry in Tyler's voice had me smirking for an instant until I thought about the things he'd been exposed to and decided I was being cruel.

I pulled a cutting board out of a cabinet and retrieved a knife from the block, placing everything on the kitchen island before I grabbed the bag of produce and Italian sausage we'd picked up at the grocery. We were making an Italian sausage bake I'd found on a recipe website. It looked easy enough for the two of us to tackle.

"Yes. My name is Mosby Leslie. I'm not in the mob either. I'm a painter, or I used to be. Hell, I don't even know anymore."

That caught his attention. "Can you reach into the cabinet behind you and grab a colander?" I opened the cloth bag and removed the produce for Tyler to clean while I began to sauté the sausage.

"Like houses?"

I chuckled. "It would have been easier, I'm certain. I probably should have been clearer with you. I paint... Come with me."

I took his hand and led him upstairs to my studio. Before I opened the door, I turned to Tyler and smiled. "This is my studio. It's very messy, but I like it this way."

I leaned forward and pecked his lips while I reached behind my back and turned the knob. The room was warm, and the sun shone through the curtainless windows. I scanned the space trying to take in what he saw, and there, on the easel, was the half-finished painting of Tyler.

"Is that how you see me?" He pointed to the canvas.

I stared at it, seeing the slight pink hue I'd added to his cheeks to highlight his beauty. The only thing really missing was his eyes because I wanted to get the color just right.

His irises were lighter than I remembered, but there was more sunlight in this room than there had been in his bedroom when I'd spent the night. "Hang on. Don't go anywhere."

I hurried downstairs and turned off the boiling water on the stove. I hadn't turned on the burner with the sausage yet, so I stuck the pan into the fridge in order not to kill us by food poisoning. I grabbed a stool from the island and hurried back upstairs to the studio.

"Okay, will you give me half an hour? Take a seat." I put the stool in a spot to get the best light possible, and I began mixing paint as I stared at Tyler.

"Can you turn a little to your right?" He did as I asked.

"That's perfect. So, anyway, I destroyed a commission I painted for a client because my boyfriend died. Well, that's not exactly right, either. He committed suicide. He was cheating with someone, and that guy got killed in an accident on a movie set, so Alistaire took a boat out for a joy ride and jumped in Lake Michigan. He drowned. He couldn't swim. Chin up, please."

Tyler lifted his chin. "I'm sorry." His voice was soft, and I knew I'd told the story in the most fucked-up way possible. In fact, I sounded like a callous jackass.

I stood from my stool and placed the palette on top. I walked over to where he was sitting and took his hands in mine, putting his palms flat on my chest. "That came out really horrible, I know. I'm sorry. Alistaire Scott was his name. We'd been together for ten years. We owned a house together in California, and I bought out his half and sent his things to his parents after he died.

"I was a real mess, and I couldn't pull my head out of my ass while I was surrounded by everything we'd built together. I came up here, and I've been hiding for a year. I saw you the day I fell and wanted to get to know you.

Telling you I couldn't remember my name or where I lived seemed the best way to be around you. I'm sorry I lied. I'd been painting that morning, which is why I looked like a vagrant, and I've been letting my hair and beard grow so nobody recognizes me."

Tyler stared at me for a moment, so I released his hands. He didn't move them an inch. "I don't lie. I'm the guy who drove the robbers to the sheriff's office, remember? I respect your privacy and won't tell anyone who you are, but please don't lie to me again. It got me in trouble in the past, and I've promised myself I won't tolerate liars anymore."

He quickly pulled his hands from my chest and glanced at the floor. I squatted a bit and looked into his beautiful brown eyes with the gold flecks finally gazing into mine. "You have my word. I will never lie to you again. Promise."

Then, like a total douche, I held out my pinky like I remembered the girls doing in grade school—which was a hell of a long time ago. "Pinky swears."

Tyler grinned at me and his whole face lit up. He held out his pinky. "Pinky swears."

I kissed him again and went back to the canvas. Tyler kept his gaze on me as I painted his eyes the perfect shade of brown with those little golden sparkles. Once the eyes were exactly as I wanted them, I put the brush in the jar on the paint-splattered table and wiped the palette with the shop towels I used upstairs, tossing them into the trash.

I took Tyler's hand and led him out of the room and downstairs. "Let's fix something to eat. So, do you know how to sauté sausage?" He released the most amazing giggle, and I was hooked. Just one giggle, and I was gaga for the guy.

We made dinner using the marinara sauce I'd canned and sliced peppers and onions. I boiled some ziti, not ready to tackle making pasta just yet. Maybe next time.

After we ate, I built a small fire for ambiance, not heat, and we sat in the living room. "How'd you learn to do that?" He was pointing to the crackling fireplace, making the room glow.

"My granddad taught me a long time ago. The house doesn't have a furnace, which makes it really fucking cold in the winter. He said if I was going to spend time at the cabin, I needed to know how to keep myself warm. He said if he came up here and found me frozen solid, he'd be pissed."

Another giggle. I relaxed on the couch and pulled Tyler on top of me. He relaxed with his head on my chest, and I played with his hair. "I'm inexperienced, Les—Mosby. That's actually a cool name. Is it a family name?"

I kissed the top of his head. "My nana's maiden name, actually. Look, I'm fine with inexperience, Tyler. We can see what we like and what we don't. There's no rush for anything to happen between us, but if something makes you uncomfortable, or if you don't want to do something because of what happened when you...uh..." Yeah, I was rambling.

Tyler propped himself up on my chest, left hand holding up his head. "This is probably none of my business, so tell me if you don't want to answer, okay?"

I gave him a small smile as I twisted a lock of his brown hair through my fingers. "Ask away."

"How old are you?"

"Thirty-nine. You're twenty-three, right?"

"I'll be twenty-four on July fifth. When is your birthday?" Tyler was combing through my beard. It was relaxing.

"It was February 28. I don't celebrate it, really. Haven't celebrated since Alistaire and I started dating. He was two years older than me, and it bothered him that he was aging. I mean, we all are fucking aging, aren't we?"

"Kinda hard not to. Would you be offended if we celebrated your birthday after the fact?"

I moved my hands to the small of his back and rubbed my fingers over the top of his sexy ass. "Like what kind of celebrate?"

Tyler giggled again, and his body squirmed on top of me, his hard cock rubbing against mine through our clothes. I wanted to flip us and grind my cock into his, but I wouldn't do that to him. We'd go at his pace—even if it killed me.

Chapter Eleven
Tyler

"Just dinner. Maybe cake to celebrate your birthday? My mom's a great cook, and maybe she can teach us some recipes. Nothing formal, I promise. You in? There's a huge reason, I believe, to celebrate that you were born."

I buried my face in his neck and nipped, bringing a groan from Mosby. It would take some time to get used to his real name, but I was thrilled he trusted me enough to tell me the truth.

To be honest, art wasn't anything I knew much about. I wasn't sophisticated like other folks who loved it because my art education was limited. It wasn't anyone's fault, it just was.

Seeing the picture of me in his studio had taken my breath away. Sitting on the stool so he could get my eyes the way he wanted in the painting had been a rush, but I hadn't wanted to sound like a naïve little dimwit, so I'd kept my mouth shut and let the man do what he wanted.

"Mmmm. As much as I'm enjoying this, I need to take you home. Do you work tomorrow? Do you want to do something when you finish?" *Yes, and please!*

"Yeah. I work until six tomorrow night and close the shop. The cleaning crew comes through overnight on Saturday and does the deep clean, so I only need to empty trash and clean out the fridge. I can be ready by six thirty. I wish you didn't have to come get me. Maybe I can get Mom to bring me?" I hated that I couldn't have a driver's license, but Mosby knew why, and he didn't seem put off by it.

"I'll be there at six and help you. Maybe we can order from that pizza place between Foggy Basin and Miller's Point? I've picked up pizza from there before, and it's damn good." Mosby flipped around and picked me up, making me laugh as I latched onto his neck to keep from falling.

"I'm a pizza snob, so it better be good." I giggled again as Mosby popped me on the butt with his right hand and tossed me over his shoulder to carry me to the door. It was the sexiest thing that had ever happened to me.

It was April in Northern California, and we were going through a dry spell. A few ski areas near Mount Shasta were still open, but our small mountain was dry and warm during the day. It was still cool in the evenings here and there, but the trees were budding, and it wouldn't take long before everything would come to life. It had been years since I'd seen the mountain in spring.

Mosby opened the back door for a second before he took my coat off the hook. "This is the only coat you have?"

"I have a parka for the winter, but it's April. The weather changes fast. This is my spring coat. It's fine." He shook his head and grabbed a cotton scarf from a coat tree, wrapping it around my neck after I slid on my sneakers. He held my coat up for me, and I pushed my arms inside.

"Zip up." He put on his loafers and grabbed his leather jacket from the hook, slipping it on. He closed the doors of the fireplace and grabbed his keys.

"Ready?" He zipped my jacket all the way up and adjusted the scarf. It was absolutely the sweetest thing anyone had done for me since I was a little boy.

"I am. Thank you for the fantastic evening. I had a very good time."

"Great first date: check!" Mosby made the checkmark sign with his finger, and my heart pounded. It was wonderful to hear him say it had been a date.

He ushered me out the door and held my hand. He led me to the truck and opened the passenger side door, closing it once I was inside.

Jogging around the front of his Bronco, Mosby hopped in and quickly started the truck. "It heats up pretty quickly."

"Do you miss Alistaire?" I wanted to smack myself in the mouth for saying the words out loud. I'd been wondering about their connection since I'd heard about the man, all the while knowing it really wasn't my business.

Mosby backed up the hill to turn around in his driveway. "Not really, but it's taken a while. I let guilt make me believe Alistaire and I were madly in love, but the truth was any affection we had for each other died a while before his death. We'd tried to rekindle it when I went to New York with him, or so I thought, but it was just him setting the stage for his exit—that sounds cold. I mean for him to leave me, not kill himself. I think we were just too lazy to untangle it until he met Tariq."

When we got to the bottom of the hill, I unbuckled my seatbelt. "How do I open the padlock on the chain? You know, if someone really wanted to get in, they'd probably be able to cut the lock."

He laughed. "It's a combination lock. Four-three-two-one. I don't think anyone would try to break in, but they won't find shit if they do. It's there to keep my shrew of an agent out if she ever hunts me down. She would never figure out how to work a combination lock. I do appreciate your concern. Will you worry about me now?" Mosby turned to me and batted his eyelashes.

I laughed and opened the gate for him, closing it after he drove through. I hopped back into the Bronco and once I buckled my seatbelt, we were off.

We listened to soft R&B music on the way to Foggy Basin. Mosby turned down the alley behind the salon and parked in the delivery bay. He turned off the Bronco, and I wasn't sure what to do.

Mosby grabbed me around the waist and pulled me closer. "Back in the day when I was in high school, we made out in the car a little bit before we said goodnight."

I giggled. "Were you dating guys or girls?"

Mosby nuzzled into my neck. "Both. I am not a gold-star gay. Back in high school, I believed I was bisexual and dated girls because I thought I'd disappoint my parents if I didn't. Damn, you smell good."

His beard tickled, but I wouldn't say a word. I worried I'd combust if he kept it up, but it was a chance I was willing to take. Mosby's lips on my neck, teasing little nibbles up the side and behind my ear, gave me goosebumps.

"It's just my shampoo. Was there a special girl?"

The handsome man stopped what he was doing—which made me sad—and pulled away from me to look into my eyes. "Okay. There was a girl named Sandy. She was a cheerleader, and she had big boobs, which did nothing for me, but the other guys were jealous. We played out the typical teenage cliché and had sex on prom night of my junior year. I faked it. I had a hard time keeping up appearances, but I suspect she faked it too. I ended up dating her ex-boyfriend the summer after high school graduation. We bonded over the fact that Sandy had no gaydar." He chuckled, which did funny things to my insides.

"You heartbreaker. Why did you break up?" Obviously, he wasn't still with her. It was a safe question, I figured.

"Sandy went into the Navy after graduation, while I went to college at UC-Berkeley. My parents died in a car accident during my second year of undergrad, but I stayed in school. I met Alistair at a gallery in West Hollywood.

We moved in together a month later. I don't know what happened to Sandy."

Mosby raised an eyebrow as he stared into my eyes, the light over the back door illuminating the cab of the Bronco. "Now you. You said no boyfriend, but did you fool around with a cute boy under the football bleachers?"

My turn to laugh. "No. As I said, the boys in my school weren't exactly to my liking. I guess I was holding out for a sexy older guy who's mature but still knows how to have fun."

"Ha! Touché!" With that, he kissed me so hotly that my toes curled in my sneakers. His tongue made two passes over my lips before my brain kicked in and I opened to accept him inside.

He tasted like the pasta we'd shared, but thankfully, my mouth was the same. We played a little cat and mouse, his tongue dipping into my mouth and moving away to lead mine into his. My dick pushed against the zipper of my skinny jeans, making me pleasantly uncomfortable.

When we broke the kiss, I pulled away, breathless. "Do you wanna come up?"

His eyes studied me before he smiled. "That's very tempting, but I need to get home. I have some things to do tomorrow. Can I get a raincheck for tomorrow night? I'll bring underwear this time, I promise."

I cracked up, and Mosby chuckled with me. Once I calmed, I placed a soft kiss on his lips. "Deal. Thank you again for the wonderful evening. Be safe going home."

Mosby opened his door and got out, extending his hand to me. I slid behind the wheel and hopped out. He led me to the stairs, climbing slowly. "When you go inside, lock the door and put that gorgeous ass right to bed. Text me tomorrow and tell me what toppings you want on your pizza, and I'll pick it up on my way here."

He then wrapped me in his arms and kissed me again. It was a proper goodnight kiss, based on what I'd seen on television. As he pulled away, his hands gently squeezed my ass cheeks. "I'll see you tomorrow night at six. Sweet dreams."

I floated into the apartment, locked the door as he'd instructed, and went to bed. That night, my dreams were saccharine-sweet.

Friday morning, I awoke in a panic. I knew the fundamentals of sex between men, but I needed a bit more detailed information. Porn on the internet wasn't helpful because it showed nothing about what should happen before the couple fucked. It started with sex most of the time, and that wasn't helpful in my situation.

There was no way I could talk to my mother about anything of the sort, nor could I ask any of the women at the shop, though I was being sexist with my assumption that none of them would have a clue of the preparation required for anal sex. I really didn't want to know if they knew or not.

I got up, showered, and dressed. I had my weekly call with my therapist that I'd nearly forgotten, and when I hung up, I felt fantastic.

I went downstairs and unlocked the salon, checking that the supplies at everyone's station were filled and ready for business. I put on the coffee and checked that we had creamers. I quickly ran to the grocery store next door to pick up cucumbers and lemons for the waters we offered. I then swung by the wine aisle and picked a bottle of cabernet, not that I really knew anything about wine, but I was sure it was probably more Mosby's taste than beer. I then proceeded to the checkout to see Mr. Willis with his usual frown.

"Good morning, Mr. Willis." I was flying too high for the man to bring me down.

"Tyler. That man you were in here with yesterday, what's his name?" Mr. Willis's voice had an innate bitterness to it. *How old was he when it started sounding like that?*

Now I had a dilemma on my hands. I didn't lie. After being in prison, I knew how much trouble lying could get me in, but Mosby had told me he was hiding out. I'd never break his confidence, so I'd tap-dance around the truth.

"Leslie. His name is Leslie, why?" *See, not a lie.*

"I'm going to talk to Sheriff West about him. I think he's trouble. The sheriff needs to investigate him. Where does he live? You shouldn't be keeping company with another felon."

That was worrisome. I did my best to steer clear of the sheriff for obvious reasons, but I was sure Mosby wouldn't want Sheriff West looking into his background either. "I don't know where he lives, but I think it's best if we both mind our own business."

I paid him and grabbed my purchases, not needing a bag. I stormed out of the store and took the wine up to my place, shoving it into the fridge before I went to the shop. Mom was on the phone as I stomped to the kitchen and began angrily chopping cucumbers. I put them in the large pitcher and filled it with filtered water.

I placed the cucumber water in the refrigerator and began slicing lemon for the other pitcher. Why did people think it was okay to get into everyone's business? I'd spent the last six months of my freedom being talked down to by people like Mr. Willis. I was damn sick and tired of it.

Mom came into the kitchen. "Good morning, sweetheart. How are you today?" She pecked a kiss on my cheek, and then she stopped. "What's wrong? Your energy is off."

I wanted to smile, but I was too pissed. "Mr. Willis is a douchebag." I tried to be a nice person, but sometimes it was impossible.

"That stupid old man. What did he say?"

I put the knife down and turned, seeing her concern. She'd been so happy when she left the previous evening. I didn't want to ruin her mood too.

"Nothing new. So, uh, I have a favor. Remember Leslie? The guy who tripped on the step?"

Mom nodded. "He doesn't have a residual issue related to the fall, does he?"

I poured Mom a cup of coffee. "No, no. He's really nice. We hung out together last night, and I found out his birthday was a few weeks ago, and he didn't celebrate. I was thinking maybe we could make him dinner tomorrow night, and you could help me make him a birthday cake. I'll get the groceries for it if you'll help me."

Mom smiled, and I was happy to see it. She'd always been my ray of sunshine, and it was a relief my fuck up hadn't dimmed her light.

"Based on what you just said about George, I better get the groceries. I'm assuming you want to have him over to my place, right?" I nodded.

"Okay. What time tomorrow night? I only have one appointment at noon, so I can get the groceries in the morning, and we can make the cake tomorrow afternoon."

I kissed her cheek. "Thank you, Mom." The bell over the front door rang, and our day began, but I had wonderful things to look forward to for the weekend. It had been a long time since I'd been excited about anything.

At lunchtime, I walked down the block to Blue Star Diner, and while I ate the best roast beef of my life, I decided to make a call I was dreading. On and off all morning, I'd been doing research regarding anal intercourse, and I'd worked myself into a damn panic. I was sure if I told Mosby I wasn't ready, he'd be sweet about it and agree, but damn, I *was* ready. It was just the mechanics of it that was freaking me out.

I returned to the salon early and went out to the alley. I sat in the lawn chair, dialing Ramon's number. It rang twice. "Hey, Tyler. How are you, man?"

Friday the truck was in Miller's Point, so it wasn't as if I could go talk to him in person. "I'm good, Ramon. Do you have a minute to talk, or are you in the middle of the lunch rush?"

"No, I'm good, mi amigo. What's up? Oh, German looked for you on social media to leave a review, but he couldn't find your profile anywhere."

I wasn't on social media because I didn't want any of the guys that I'd known in prison to find me. I didn't think I'd done anything they'd retaliate for, but one could never be too cautious.

"Yeah, uh, I'll keep that in mind. Can I talk to you about something kind of embarrassing?"

It was suddenly quiet on Ramon's end of the line. "Sure. I just walked away from the truck. What's up? You okay?"

I chuckled. "I'm panicked. I, uh, I'm a virgin." I waited to get his reaction to that information.

"Good for you. You waited for someone special to take that step with. It's not a bad thing, Tyler."

That was reassuring to hear. "No, I know that. The issue is, I've found that guy. He's incredible. He's funny. He's kind. He treats me like I'm important, so I believe he's special, and I want to take that step with him. I just don't know how."

Silence. The heat rose up my chest to the top of my head in record time. I was sure I was glowing.

"Okay, explain a little more, please. I want to answer your questions. I just don't know if I'm the right person."

"I, uh, I'm sorry. This was a mistake." I started to hang up, but...

"Wait. German, babe."

I put the phone back to my ear and walked to the end of the alley, staring into space. People everywhere fucked. It couldn't be that hard to figure it out, right?

"Hello?" It wasn't Ramon.

"German? How's your hair? Any complaints?"

"Not at all, Tyler. I wanted to ask if you have business cards or if it's okay if I just give out your cell number? Oh, should I give them the number for Shear Bliss?"

I responded with a nervous giggle. There were other people who wanted me to cut their hair? That seemed like a dream.

"Oh, uh, I don't have a business card yet. You can go ahead and give them my cell number. I don't have a book, so I'm making my own appointments right now."

"Oh, cool. Let me know if it's too much. I have a lot of family, and when I told them about the— Uh, what? Oh? Oh! Alright. So, uh, Tyler, I'm sorry. What can I explain to you? Ramon told me you have some questions. I'll tell you everything I can."

Tears filled my eyes. I sobbed, hard. I wasn't sure if it was embarrassment or gratitude. "I, uh, I don't want to disappoint the guy I'm interested in. I've never had sex before, and I have no"—*sob!*—"idea what I'm doing." I felt stupid.

"Where are you?" German sounded worried.

"I'm not driving or anything. I'm on my break. I'm sitting behind the salon. I'm sorry. You're probably really busy. I shouldn't have bothered you guys."

"No, no. What time do you finish work?"

"We close at six. My boyfriend—I mean, the guy I'm seeing—is coming here at six."

"Okay, well we finish here at three and cleanup takes an hour. I'll drop by at four-thirty, and we'll talk. I mean, if you can get away for a few minutes. I promise you're psyching yourself out, which won't help. Calm down, take a few breaths, and we'll talk about it at four-thirty."

"Thank you. I appreciate this. Your next trim is on me."

German laughed. "Sure. See you later."

We ended the call, and I snuck into the salon restroom. My eyes were a little puffy and red, but I had a sense of calm I hadn't expected. After I splashed cold water on my face, I barely looked like I'd been crying.

Everything was going to be just fine...or it was all going straight to hell on a rollercoaster...

The day was crazy busy with hair emergency after hair emergency.

"Is there something in the water? What are these women doing?" Camila breezed by me with a bowl of hair color for a client who had gone to Mexico with gorgeous blonde and platinum highlights and returned with a mop of pea-green straw.

I glanced at the clock to see it was ten after four. "If I put that on your client's hair, will you cover for me? I'm meeting a friend upstairs for a quick pep talk, and then I'll be back to finish the day, I swear."

Camila looked me up and down. "Is it that cute guy who fell? If you talk him into a haircut and a shave, I think you'll find a really hot guy under there. I'll cover and close for you tonight. I have nothing going on. I'll tell your mother you weren't feeling well, and I'm staying to cover for you."

I flung myself at her, nearly knocking the bowl out of her hands. "Thank you. I owe you a lot for this, Camila. Thank you so much."

She laughed and handed me the bowl, and I hurried out to her chair where the twenty-ish young woman was furiously texting on her sparkling smartphone. "Hi. I'm Tyler. I'll be applying the color to your hair. Camila mixed it. She's taking a call, but she'll be back."

The woman glanced at me, flipped her hand, and shoved earbuds into her ear as her phone rang. I took that as a yes.

If applying corrective color was an Olympic sport, I would be proudly standing on the center platform having achieved a new world record. Once the color was applied and combed through, I put the mane up in a plastic clip and grabbed the tools to sterilize them. I quickly turned on the timer, laid it on the counter by the mirror, and hurried back to the kitchen.

"She's all set. I turned on the timer for fifteen minutes, but I think you might need to give it another round because under the top layer of highlights is a seaweed color, which leads me to believe she tried to fix it herself first and messed up the low lights."

Camila and Alice both looked at me. "What?" Did I fart?

"You know about coloring hair?"

I was a little offended. "Yeah. What? You don't think I actually went to cosmetology school? I didn't study make-up, though I know how to apply a smokey eye better than either of you. I know everything you know, and I've had over a thousand clients for the last three-and-a-half years." I looked out the window to see German parking out front. "Bye."

I took off my apron and put it on my chair before I left. I met German on the sidewalk and directed him around to the stairs. We hurried up, and I let us inside. "Where's Ramon? He knows you're here, right?" God, I had enough of my own drama. I didn't need to start more with newlyweds.

German chuckled. "He took the truck home. He knows exactly where I am and what I'm doing. Now." German put a brown bag on the table and scooted it over to me. I stared at it for a moment like it contained a rattlesnake, and then I opened it.

I reached inside and found lube—three different kinds, which was two more than I'd ever thought about. Guys in prison used anything slick from hair conditioner to bacon grease smuggled from the kitchen in foil that you could trade for canteen snacks. Everybody had an agenda.

"Why three?" I put them on the table and pulled out a chair. German sat across from me and picked up the first one. "This is an oil-based lube. It's coconut oil and smells nice. It's great for playing around. Fingers inside, masturbation, frottage. Oil-based lubes are thicker and more viscous, but they will destroy a condom."

He put down that bottle and picked up the second. "This is a silicone-based lube. It's good to use with condoms and any toys you'd like to use except silicone. It will mess them up pretty bad, as Ramon and I learned the hard way until we did the damn research. Water-based lube is best with silicone toys, but you can use silicone lube with glass or metal toys."

As enlightening as all of it was, I had one distinct issue. "Thanks. I haven't used toys or anything. Hell, I haven't been fucked yet, which is what I hope happens tonight, so, uh…" My voice was a little harsher than I intended, but the anxiety was killing me.

I reached into the bag again and pulled out two boxes of condoms. "These I know about."

I reached into the bag and pulled out the last thing inside—a black rubber thing with a tubelike tip. I glanced at it and then lifted my eyes to German.

He offered a kind smile. "That's an enema bulb. Now, before you panic, let me dissuade you of the fear of crapping the bed. That's only happened to me about a dozen times."

My eyes grew ten times their regular size before German started cracking up. "Sorry, just a little potty humor Ramon dared me to use. So, let's talk about bodily functions."

Fifteen minutes later, I knew how poop worked—I'd never bothered to look it up because it just happened, but wow. The shit—pardon the pun—I hadn't known could have filled a series of books.

"Last thing, and I'll get out of here. Don't go too fast the first time, and if he's a good guy like you claim, he won't push you to do more than you're ready for. And you might not have an orgasm during penetration, but don't freak out. Look, Ty, it's a big step, and if you're not ready and your guy is decent, he'll wait as long as it takes. Now, use warm water in this,"—he picked up the blub thing—"and stick close to the toilet. A few good flushes, and you'll be golden if you want to go through with it." He put the bulb on the table and stared at me with a kind smile.

"Thank you, German, so much. I really appreciate your help."

He nodded. "Drop me a text tomorrow and let me know you're okay. Here's my number." He handed me a business card for the food truck with his and Ramon's numbers on it.

"And it's cool that you didn't ask, but I'll tell you. Ramon and I are verse. He's just too shy to explain things like this. His family was hard on him when he first came out, and it's still weird for them. My family, however, has been great about it. Did I tell you I grew up with two moms?"

We both laughed, and German gave me a hug. I walked him through the room and opened the door for him to leave. There, standing on my little porch, was none other than Mosby Leslie.

Shit!

No pun intended...

Chapter Twelve
Mosby

I parked at the public lot across the street, grabbed the pizza, and walked up to the salon. Tyler hadn't texted with what he liked on his pizza, so I took a guess. If he didn't like it, I'd buy a box of cereal from the fucking grocery store, and we'd eat the whole damn thing.

Looking in through the window, I didn't see Tyler anywhere. A beautiful black woman was at the register chatting with Tyler's mother, so I went inside.

The little bell almost sounded like Big Ben in my head. Everyone looked up at the same time, and the place went quiet—like a tomb.

Tyler's mom grinned at me, as did the woman next to her who I remembered vaguely from the day I cracked my head. "Well, well, if it isn't the tripper. Are you here to let me clean up that mess on your face, honey? I like the hair, though it needs a trim. Those dead ends are tragic."

I chuckled. "If anyone is going to touch my hair, it will be Tyler. Is he here? We're supposed to clean up the salon and have pizza."

"Oh. Leslie. I'm afraid Tyler isn't feeling well," his mother said. She was staring at me pretty intensely, too.

The beautiful Latina I'd met at the produce stand stepped closer. "Actually, I think he's waiting for you upstairs." She winked. Tyler must have told her about us.

"Thank you." I headed back out and around the corner seeing the little heart I'd drawn in the cement when it was wet. One day I'd have to confess to defacing their property, but I wanted to mark the spot where I looked into those gorgeous brown eyes for the first time.

I went around the side of the building and took the stairs two at a time. When I reached the top, I was poised to knock when the door opened. Standing in front of me was a handsome guy who wasn't Tyler. He had shoulder-length dark brown hair, and a warm smile.

"Hello there. Is Tyler—" Suddenly, Tyler appeared next to the guy, his face beet red.

"Mo—Leslie. Come in, please. This is German, my friend. He was just leaving." He turned to the guy, and they shared a quick hug. The guy slid out the door and stepped close in front of me.

German was a big bastard, for sure. "If you hurt him, I will find you." Without another word he ran down the steps and got into a black pickup that could have been the grandson of my old Bronco.

I stepped inside and closed the door. I started to put the pizza on the table when I saw what was laid out on top of it.

"Did I break up a really lowkey sex-toy party?" There on the table were three bottles of lube, two boxes of condoms, and an enema bulb. There was a paper bag from the drugstore in Miller's Point, where I'd stopped a few times.

I picked up the condoms. One was lambskin and the other was polyurethane. Both were multipacks with varied sizes. "I prefer these in case you're interested." I held up the lambskin box.

"Uh, Mosby, German was… I mean, we didn't… He's married to Ramon. Ramon is Camila's brother. They own a food truck that—"

That was where I recognized the guy from. I'd stopped at the truck a time or two when I found it on Tuesdays in Veterans Park. "Ah, that's where I recognized him from. Anyway, what did I interrupt?"

Tyler sighed. "I called him in a panic because I don't know how to have sex."

That wasn't what I expected. "So, he came to *show* you?"

My gut turned at the thought of Tyler with another man. In my heart I knew he wasn't like Alistaire. Hell, he was the polar opposite of Alistaire. I could see Tyler's fingers twisting together, so I tossed the condoms on the table and stepped closer to him.

"I want you to know that you can come to me with any questions. You told me you're a virgin, and I'm not going to rush you, sweetheart."

Tyler put his hands on my chest. "I don't want to be bad at it, Mosby. I don't want you to give up on me because I don't know what I'm doing. You… You were with someone for ten years, and here I am, this guy who has never had anybody want to—"

I pulled him closer and kissed the end of his cute nose. "Bunny, we have a whole life ahead of us to figure things out. I understand that there might be things you don't feel comfortable talking to me about just yet. You're young, and you haven't had a lot of the experiences I've had, but I hope we'll get to the point where you aren't worried about discussing anything."

My palm touched his jaw, feeling a little stubble along his jawline and the beginnings of a mustache. He looked more adorable than I remembered from the night before, or maybe it was just that I realized I could be falling in love with him. Was the insta-love thing Alistaire mentioned in his now-cinders diary a real thing?

"You called me Bunny?" He grinned and kissed me, which I truly enjoyed.

"I might unless you have a strong objection. You remind me of a cute little rabbit that I've seen up in the woods behind the cabin. Barbara Bushy scares it away when it tries to come close."

"I've been called a lot worse. So, you're an animal lover?" He slid his hands under my jacket and pushed it off my shoulders.

I hated taking my hands off him, so I quickly let him go, draped my leather jacket over the back of his kitchen chair, and wrapped him up in my arms again, glancing at the table. "I love certain animals. Not a fan of spiders or snakes, but I believe in a peaceful co-existence. So, that black woman at the salon who told me that the ends of my hair were tragic? What's her name?"

Tyler giggled. "Edina. She didn't mean anything by it. She's worked for my mom for a long time, and she is really a wonderful person. She's very protective of Mom and me. I-I just wanted not to look stupid."

I took his hand and led him to his couch, sitting and pulling him onto my lap—something Alistaire would never agree to do. "You could never look stupid to me, Bunny. You're handsome, kind, generous. I can keep searching for adjectives if you'd like."

He giggled again, his sexy ass rubbing against my very hard cock, which was dying to make an appearance. I could control myself, but that didn't mean we wouldn't explore if he was willing.

"Okay, after talking to German, how do you feel about intercourse? We're not going to do anything you don't want tonight, but I'd love to feel your skin next to mine."

Tyler glanced at the pizza on the table. "If we're not going to have sex, can we eat the pizza?"

I had to laugh. "Did you not eat today?"

Tyler glanced up at me through his lashes. "I was too excited and worried, but now I'm starving."

I stood with him in my arms. "Let's see if we need to heat it up." I carried him to the kitchen area, and he pulled out a round pizza pan. We put the pie on it and Tyler turned on the oven to warm.

"How was your day?" Tyler was standing with that sexy ass sticking out of the fridge.

My brain immediately went into overdrive to the point I thought I'd have to slam my dick in a fucking drawer to get it under control. "It was pretty good. I finished the picture of you and decided it was terrible, so I primed and sanded the canvas to use again. I'm thinking of taking up glass blowing."

Tyler came out of the fridge with a bottle of red wine, which gave me pause. When I glanced at him, I saw that he was excited, so I kept my mouth shut. I glanced at the bottle to see it wasn't a familiar brand, but again, I said nothing.

Tyler opened the cabinet next to the refrigerator and pulled down two white wine glasses and put them on the table. "Do you like red? I was trying to figure out what you might like to drink. I wasn't sure if you were a beer guy because you're so sophisticated."

I nodded. "Where's your wine opener?" I could drink cold cabernet. Alistaire, though, would be spinning in his grave if I'd presented the same to him.

"Oh. I don't have one. The cap screws off." Tyler took the bottle and ripped off the seal. He then opened the metal cap and poured me a full glass of wine before I could stop him.

He poured a little in his own glass, leaving me to wonder how I could choke down a full glass of cold, cheap cabernet. "Thank you."

"Do you mind eating off paper plates? It'll make cleanup much easier."

Plates were never meant to be paper unless they were for feeding a squirrel. Eating a meal off them—even if it was pizza—felt blasphemous, especially with the way Alistaire and I had lived our lives.

"Paper plates are just fine. No problem." I wasn't with Alistaire any longer. I was with my beautiful Bunny, and I had to let thoughts of Alistaire go. My life wasn't that way any longer.

I sipped my wine and did my best to hide the sneer. It wasn't good. I hadn't had anything stronger than beer since I'd arrived in Foggy Basin. I'd checked out the wine selection at the grocery store and found it severely lacking, so I'd stuck with beer—in a bottle, not a can. God, I'd become a snob and hated it.

"So, uh, do you like wine?" I stared at him, trying to judge his interest. If he liked it, I'd find something we could drink without it tasting like poison.

"This is the first time I've had it. Seventeen in prison, remember? My mom likes white zinfandel, but I thought you'd like something that didn't come in a box. Camila drinks red wine over ice. Would you like some ice?"

God, he was trying so hard to impress me, and I felt like such a fucking judgmental dick. "Uh, does she drink sangria? Red wine with fruit and a little tequila or vodka?" I loved Spanish and Mexican cuisines, and I knew sangria was delicious.

"Oh, uh, she just calls it red wine, but maybe that's what she means. I, uh, I can go to the grocery store and get some fruit and do it that way if you want."

Tyler got up and started for the door, but I caught him. "It's fine. I just want to spend time with you. I'll have water with the pizza. So, let's play twenty questions." We walked over to the small table and sat.

"Okay. Uh, what's your favorite TV show?" He was flashing that smile my way again. He had no idea the power he had over me.

I didn't watch television. I didn't even have one at the cabin or in the Montecito house. I much preferred to read or paint when I had free time. "I, uh, don't watch television. I used to watch Looney Tunes when I was a kid."

His eyes lit up. "What's Looney Tunes?"

I chuckled and took another sip of the cold cabernet. "Cartoons. Daffy Duck and Bugs Bunny?"

He giggled. "I think I've seen some of those. I didn't realize they were that old." He stared at me before he opened his mouth and put his hand over it. That made me laugh.

"You're so damn cute. Do you know that?" I took another swig of the terrible wine. I could learn to drink cold red if I did it with Tyler Rockwell, I was sure.

After we ate pizza, Tyler wrapped the two pieces left over and I took the trash out to the dumpster behind the salon. I noticed a guy walking down the alley, checking out the neighborhood. I slowly climbed the stairs and watched as he crossed the street to the public parking lot, stopping by my Bronco and taking a picture of the license plate.

"*Hey! I'll beat your ass!*" I shouted from the top step of Tyler's apartment. The door opened, and he came out with a mini baseball bat. "What are you going to do with that?"

I took the bat and gently pushed him back inside. "Is this your weapon of choice?"

Tyler smirked. "I'm not a violent person. Camila gave it to me to carry when I work late in the salon and walk up here alone. I don't know what kind of crime she thought I'd encounter that the little bat would scare them away."

"It was some guy taking a picture of my Bronco. Idiot. I've got a tracking device on it. I could find it in five minutes. Let's keep playing our game. My turn."

We sat on the small couch, and I pulled his legs over my lap. "If you could go anywhere in the world, where would you want to go?"

Tyler sipped his cold red and smiled. It was kind of growing on me, so I gulped a little more of mine while waiting for his response. I studied him for a moment before I put my glass on the side table and took his right hand, twining our fingers together.

"I, uh, I can't leave Foggy Basin for three years, but if I could—"

That was news, and I needed to know more—my business or not. "Why can't you leave Foggy Basin?" I pulled him onto my lap and took his hands in my left one as I wrapped my right arm around him. He looked worried, but he shouldn't have.

"It's okay. Just tell me."

"I'm required to stay in Foggy Basin as part of my parole agreement. I have therapy sessions every Friday morning, and then my therapist reports to the parole board. Once a month, I sit down with Sheriff West for a twenty-minute conversation about what's going on in my life, and then he sends an email to my parole officer in Sacramento that I'm still here and am a productive member of society."

That was a surprise to me. My involvement with law enforcement was limited. When my parents were killed, the offending driver died at the same time. I didn't get caught doing shit when I was in college, and my granddad made sure I knew he'd have my ass if I got into anything serious. I knew nothing about the aftermath of prison.

"You can't go on a trip?"

Tyler shook his head. "I don't really have the money to go anywhere anyway."

"What if you stay in the state?"

He shrugged. "I don't know anybody anywhere else. I'd really have to ask. Anyway, if I could dream of going anywhere else, I think I'd like to see New York. I've seen pictures, and it looks incredible."

I thought back to the last time I was there before Alistaire died, and I seriously had no desire to go back. All that city held for me were sad memories. "You're not missing anything, I promise."

"I'm sure you're right. How about you?"

I thought for a minute. "Paris. I went there for six months to study art, and it was beautiful. The food and wine were incredible."

I turned to smile at Tyler, seeing his face was flushed. "What?"

"God, you've been to Paris and had fancy wine, and I gave you supermarket wine with a screw cap. God, I'm sorry, Mosby. If you want to leave, I understand."

He started to get up, but I held him where he was. "Bunny, there's no way I'm missing my rain check. I wanted to see you tonight, and I'm having a great time."

"Did you bring stuff for tomorrow?"

"It's in the Bronco. I'll go get it, and then maybe we can go play in your bed?"

"I can bring my bat and come with you." We both laughed as I stood and put him on the floor.

"Thank you for your offer of protection. I'll be fine. Be right back." I went to the door and stepped out, leaving it open an inch. Once I crossed the street, I hit the flashlight app on my phone and walked around my Bronco, looking under the vehicle for anything that appeared out of place. As I suspected, I found a small metal device under the front bumper that I hadn't put there. I didn't think it was big enough to be a bomb, so I left it. I'd take it off in the morning when I left for home.

I opened the Bronco and grabbed my leather bag from the back, glancing around the inside. Everything looked as it had when I'd gotten out, so I locked and closed the door before jogging across the street and up the stairs.

I let myself inside, locked the door as I slipped off my shoes, and followed the light from the back of the apartment to Tyler's bedroom. I hadn't expected the few lit candles and purple scarf over the lamp on his bedside table.

"This looks a lot different from the last time I was here." I had to tease him a little. He was standing in the middle of the room, looking very anxious. There was one way to cure that.

I dropped my duffel on the floor and stepped over to Tyler. "Are you okay?"

He gave me a nervous, hundred-watt smile. "Yes. With you, I think I'll always be better than okay."

I sunk to my knees and glanced up at him. "Take off your shirt, Bunny."

While he fumbled with the henley he was wearing, I pulled the elastic from my hair and unbuttoned his skinny jeans, kissing and nipping along the waistband.

"God, Mosby. That feels so good."

"Put your hands in my hair and hold on." I slid the zipper down, following it with my tongue to see the most beautiful happy trail. The dark hair led me exactly where I wanted to go.

I swirled my tongue around his belly button, feeling him pull my hair a little as I tugged his jeans down to find a pair of black lace briefs that had my cock throbbing behind its denim prison.

I leaned back a bit and tapped his right foot. When he held it up, I slid the pantleg off and repeated the process on the other side, tossing the jeans aside. I tugged the waistband of his briefs out and peered inside, seeing my prize.

Tyler began massaging my scalp, which felt fantastic and had the potential to put me to sleep at any other time, but his mouthwatering cock had all my attention. I reached up and slid the waistband under his balls and stuck out my tongue to catch the precum that was sliding down the crown and onto the shaft.

"Mmmm. I knew you'd taste good." I flicked my tongue over the slit and collected the pooling fluid as Tyler moaned above me.

I slid my lips over the crown and swirled my tongue to mimic a French kiss while reaching to unbuckle my belt and open my jeans to free my aching cock. My own touch was all I'd experienced for several years, but as I sucked on Tyler's dick, there was a new fervor coursing through my body.

I gave myself a tug as I worked more of Tyler's cock into my mouth, moaning against the intrusion as his fingers tugged my hair. Stroking myself had never felt this good.

"Oh god. That's...I've never..."

Tyler's half-finished sentences were cute. I reached up with my left hand, continuing to stroke myself with my right, and rolled his balls in my palm. His grip on my hair tightened before he released it and gently smoothed his fingers over my scalp.

I pushed my index and middle fingers behind his balls and slid over his taint. He squeaked and rose onto his toes, causing his cock to hit the back of my throat, engaging my gag reflex.

"Mosby, I'm so sorry. It felt good and I couldn't help—"

"No worries, Bunny. I've gotta get more comfortable." I quickly undressed until I was completely naked and then I took in the sight of Tyler standing in front of me, his eyes fixed on my hard cock. I flexed my glutes, making it bob a bit.

Tyler giggled. "Can I suck you?"

"Most certainly. I think we can make each other happy at the same time." I took his hand and led him to the bed. I laid on my back with my head on his pillow, and I helped him straddle my torso, resting my hands on his beautiful ass still covered in the lacy briefs.

"Is this okay?" Tyler licked a stripe down my shaft, causing me to lift my hips in search of his magnificent mouth.

An instant later, I was engulfed in warm, moist heat. He slowly bobbed on my shaft, flexing his hips as he greedily sucked my cock.

I reached for the waistband of his underwear and lowered it, slowly revealing his pink entrance. It was like a curtain opening on a stage. He was hairless, which I loved. All that beautiful flesh right in front of me with no barrier.

Chapter Thirteen

Tyler

I knew how to suck a dick. I'd done it a lot in prison—well, maybe not a lot. That made me sound like a whore, which I didn't really believe myself to be. But I also wouldn't label myself a victim. It was a survival method, and I did. *Take the win!*

KC taught me a few things while I shared a cell with him. I wouldn't say he was a mentor or anything, but he taught me how to maneuver tough situations when you weren't sure of the outcome. He'd also taught me to suck a dick and not puke because when he was about to come, he'd thrust harder into my mouth and make me gag. If I didn't keep going, he'd smack me. If I did and he climaxed, he'd shove me away hard so that I landed on my ass before he climbed into the bottom bunk and turned his back to me. His snores would fill the cell block within seconds.

Based on how Mosby had sucked me, I knew he wasn't selfish. He was sweet and tender, and I wanted to give him my best.

I slowly pushed down on him until the head of his cock hit the back of my throat, and then farther until the head was beyond my gag reflex. I retreated and did it again. And again. And again.

I was getting into a good rhythm but didn't expect to feel something wet and warm against my hole. I stalled with Mosby's dick in my throat, and when I felt the tickling of my rim again, I gagged. It was really embarrassing.

Mosby sat up and pulled me to sit beside him. "I'm sorry I didn't check with you first. That was inconsiderate. I'm guessing you've never had that happen before?"

There I sat with my erection slowly deflating and my briefs half-on, half-off. I wanted to sink into the mattress. "I haven't experienced a lot of things, but I'm sorry I gagged. I didn't want to stop. I would have pushed through it, but I wanted to feel what you were doing without distraction."

"Hands and knees. I'll make sure you enjoy it, Bunny, without distractions." As guilty as I felt about not finishing the blowjob, I really wanted him to do what he'd been doing.

Mosby winked and patted my leg, both of us moving around on the mattress until I was on my hands and knees, and he was behind me. He pushed my briefs farther down, and his tongue slowly circled my entrance.

"Oh god." My voice sounded choked, but the sensations racing through my body as he ate my ass were mind-numbingly perfect.

My dick sprang to life so fast I was a little lightheaded for a moment. I lost myself in the feel of his tongue breaching me, and colors swirled in front of my eyes.

A slick finger pushed inside my ass as Mosby slid under me, his head coming between my thighs as he sucked my hard-on into his mouth. And, just like that, I shot off in ten seconds. The first time I was touched in such a beautiful way where all the attention was on me, I shot off like the amateur I was.

Mosby slid through my open legs and moved to sit against the headboard, pulling me onto him and kissing me. He still had my cum in his mouth, and he shared it with me, which was the sexiest thing I'd ever done in my life.

"See. I told you that you tasted sweet. Are you okay? Was that okay?" His expression was worried.

"What you did was something I never expected would happen to me. It was beautiful, Mosby. Thank you." He pulled my briefs off and moved me on top of him as he rested on the pillows.

His hard cock was against my deflated one, and I glanced up. "I can take care of that for you."

Mosby smirked. "Stay right where you are. Holding you in my arms is more important than a hard-on. You deserve to be treated like the treasure I believe you to be. If you'll let me."

Wow!

Saturday afternoon, I closed the salon at two after Mom finished her noon appointment. After I ensured everything was ready for Monday morning, I locked up and went upstairs.

I took a quick shower and styled my hair, and for the first time in five years, I stared at my clean face. Camila had been kind enough to make a store run for me on her way to the salon to pick up a few things. I stared at the small boxes in front of me, wondering if I was making a mistake.

Earlier that morning, Mosby had gone home—after giving me a searing kiss and a pat on my bare ass as I stood by the door with him. "I can't wait to see you tonight, my beautiful Bunny." I'd been giddy the whole time I worked, and after I locked up, I'd run up the back stairs nearly wiping out twice.

I stared into the mirror after putting on the pore-reducing primer Camila had brought me—which was much more expensive than the brand I'd requested. "Are you sure you want to show this side of yourself to Mosby? What if he doesn't like the makeup?"

The unopened compacts, pencils, and jars spread out on the counter were the same products I'd used years ago in high school to hide from the world because I didn't feel good enough as myself. I had acne and a scrawny body, and I was gay. People were quite judgmental of me, with my mother being the only person who seemed to accept me back then.

The makeup gave me self-confidence and a fuck-you attitude. If people were going to talk about me behind my back, I wanted it to be because my mascara was smeared or because my perfect lip-liner was smudged. I didn't want it to be because my skin wasn't perfect and my eyes were dull and lifeless without shadow and liner.

Now, here I was at twenty-three, fearing judgment by a man I adored because I *enjoyed* wearing makeup and standing out in a crowd. Was I willing to risk Mosby walking away from me because I was the guy who wore makeup, or would he think I looked sexy?

"No time like now to find out." I picked up the concealer and began the ritual, humming along with the playlist I was listening to as I shaped my brows, highlighted my cheeks, and curled my lashes.

I skipped the foundation I used to wear because I'd finally started getting hair on my face. I let it cover my jawline because of the acne scarring, and I had a light mustache. I thought it looked good, and I liked the sheer highlighter and soft blush. A bit of eyeliner for definition and a pop of color on my lips, and I was ready to go.

Once I was satisfied, I started to flip off the light, but then a flash of fear shot through me, and I grabbed two makeup remover towelette packets and slid them into my pocket, just in case.

Wallet in my back pocket and keys in hand, I headed to my mom's. It was a nice afternoon with lots of flowering trees coming to life. It was just as I used to fantasize about when I was locked up. I was so grateful to be experiencing it in person.

I went around to the back door, seeing Mom had already pulled out the charcoal grill from the garage. We were making surf and turf with mushroom risotto. It dawned on me that I hadn't asked if Mosby had any food allergies, so I pulled out my phone.

> **Hello! I forgot to ask if you had any food allergies I should know about. I'm looking forward to seeing you.**

I started to type my name but thought better and signed the message with *Bunny*. It was cute, and I'd never had a nickname that wasn't degrading, so I was going to embrace it.

"Mom!" I went in through the back door and stepped into the kitchen to see something I'd never seen before…my mother in the arms of a tall brown-haired man holding a cowboy hat in one hand and my mother's ass in the other.

"Oh!" I quickly backed out of the kitchen and wondered what the hell was going on. A moment later, my mother stepped out, her face flushed and her eyes glazed. I chose to ignore that.

"I'm sorry, Ty. Beau surprised me. He was supposed to be moving cattle this weekend, but they decided to do it on Thursday and yesterday instead. He, uh, he's staying at the Foggy Basin Inn, so I invited him over for dinner. Come inside and meet him. He's a really nice man. I want you to be respectful to him."

My brain couldn't let go of the man's large paw on my mother's ass. I'd already formed an opinion of what type of guy he was—*handsy*.

I walked inside to see he'd hung his ten-gallon hat on the back of one of the kitchen chairs as if it was the most natural thing to do. He was leaning on the counter with his ankles and arms crossed. He stared at me, and my sassy high school queen came bounding forward.

I stuck out my hand, wishing I'd had time to paint my nails so I could freak out the judgmental prick. "Hi there. I'm Tyler Rockwell, Marlena's son."

The man stood on both feet as he stared at my mom like the cat had his tongue. "Tyler, this is Beau Fletcher. He's an old friend of mine."

I chuckled. "Understatement, Mom."

I stared at the man the same way he'd stared at me. Finally, he took my hand and gave me a nervous grin. "Tyler, it's nice to meet you, son. I've heard a lot about you."

"Uh-huh. I bet. So, uh, Mom said she invited you for dinner. I should tell you we're celebrating the birthday of the man I'm seeing." His eyes got big. "Ah, did Marlena neglect to mention I'm gay?"

"Tyler Alan Rockwell! Beau knows you're gay. Don't be so salty."

Full named. I was probably in a lot of trouble after Beau Fletcher returned to whatever bigoted rock he'd crawled out from under, but I didn't care. *Don't come on my turf and judge me.*

"I, uh, I just rolled into town, so I'm going to go to the motel and clean up. What time should I come back, Marlie?"

Ah, so he had a nickname for my mother. She giggled like a teenager. I rolled my eyes.

"We're planning to eat at five-thirty." I jutted my chest out defiantly. How dare he show up and ruin my plans.

"I'll walk you out, Beau, while Tyler looks for where he left his manners." Okay, that stung.

I opened the fridge and snagged the pitcher of lemonade, grabbing two glasses from the cabinet and filling both with ice. I poured the lemonade I knew Mom had made that morning and waited for her to come back.

She returned a minute later, looking as if she'd been put under a spell. Her blouse had been retucked, thankfully, but I knew if I'd been five-minutes later, the man would have had her naked on the kitchen table.

I glanced at the table and cringed, going to the hall closet to get the disinfectant to clean it since I had no idea if they'd already done the nasty before I arrived. Maybe he was leaving after they'd done the deed? I saturated the table and grabbed the roll of paper towels to dry it.

"What the hell's gotten into you, Tyler?" My mother never cursed, so I was caught a bit off-guard.

"This dinner is very important to me. I wanted you to get to know Leslie, and I thought a birthday celebration might be a nice thing to do for him. His parents died when he was twenty, and he usually doesn't celebrate his birthday. He has a cabin up the mountain that's been in his family for years. He's an artist and doesn't have a family to celebrate him. I wanted us to be that for him."

That was a lot more than I'd planned to share with her before talking to Mosby about what he wanted her to know, but I was hoping maybe she'd have mercy on me and uninvite her friend. Based on the look in her eyes, that wasn't going to happen.

"How old is that guy?" As I'd stared at him, I noticed his hair was grayer than I'd first thought when he was bent over my mother.

"Beau is fifty-eight. I met him years ago, and we lost touch, but he's had some changes in his life, and he called me before you were released. I made him wait to meet you until now. I expect you to show Beau the same amount of respect you want me to show Leslie."

Damn, that was dirty pool.

Chapter Fourteen
Mosby

"And you'll deliver it tonight to the address I gave you, correct? Your salesman has the note." I had a bad habit of browbeating people I did business with, and the young man from the dealership wasn't filling me with confidence that he had a handle on the task at hand.

"Yeah, man. I got it. I'll drop it off behind Shear Bliss. Put the keys in the envelope with the note and leave them on the seat. That it?"

At this point, I needed to get going if I planned to get to Foggy Basin on time. I'd researched my idea all day and confirmed it with the salesman I'd met with after I left Tyler's place that morning. It would be a miracle if it worked out, including if Tyler would accept my gift.

"Yes. That's it. If it's done properly, I'll drop off a generous tip for you tomorrow. Text me when it's been delivered." I was hoping to spend the night at Tyler's apartment, so I could run by the dealership on my way home the next day—if the kid didn't fuck it up.

We ended the call, and I gathered my things to leave. I stepped onto the porch to see Barbara Bushy sitting on the railing where I'd left her food and water. "Be good. I'll be back tomorrow."

I hurried to the Bronco and slid inside, driving down the hill to the gate. I'd left it unlocked when I returned home earlier, but now that I would be gone overnight, I would lock it. I hadn't officially been invited to spend the night, but I had high hopes.

I drove through the gate and stopped, grabbing my mail before looping the chain and engaging the padlock. I returned to the driver's seat and dropped the mail in my duffel before heading to town.

Once on the road, I glanced in the rearview mirror and thought I saw a fancy SUV following me. Since I'd left that tracking device in the public parking lot across from Shear Bliss, I'd been trying to figure out who the fuck put it on my vehicle in the first place.

Thankfully, when I made the right into town, the SUV behind me went straight. I passed the salon and made the left at Valley Way Drive, which led to Tyler's mother's house.

A huge pickup truck was parked in the driveway, so I parked on the street. As I got out of the Bronco, the door to the pickup truck opened and a tall cowboy stepped out. He must not have seen me because he put a cowboy hat on his head and then looked in the side mirror, smoothing and checking the tuck of his starched shirt.

He slid the top of his right boot over the left calf of his jeans and then repeated the process on the opposite side. I stared at the man because he looked familiar, though I couldn't place from where, so I walked around my Bronco and opened the passenger door, grabbing the potted gardenia that was just starting to bloom. I'd picked it up at a nursery near the dealership to give to Tyler's mom, hoping to make a good impression.

"Shit. I shoulda thought of that." I turned to see the cowboy staring at the plant. I had no idea who the man was, and I wasn't sure what to say to him.

"It was a miracle I thought of it, to be honest. I'm Mo-Leslie. I'm a friend of Tyler's." He stared at me before he smiled.

"I'm a friend of Marlena's. Beau Fletcher. Pleasure. It must be your birthday?" He extended his hand, and I shook it. He seemed pleasant enough.

Beau stepped onto the small porch first, and I stood on the stairs behind him. He rang the doorbell, and we glanced at each other. After a minute, the door opened, and Marlena smiled, looking beautiful in a flowered top and denim skirt. "Come in, guys."

Beau removed his hat showing off salt and pepper hair cut very short. His face was clean-shaven, and when he bent down to kiss a much-shorter Marlena, she giggled. "You smell very good."

"You too, darlin'." He stepped inside, and I stepped onto the porch.

"Ms. Rockwell, this is for you." I handed her the gardenia, and she smiled at me, making me grin in return. *Point for me.*

"Tyler, Leslie's here."

I glanced toward the kitchen to see my beautiful Bunny coming closer with a denim apron smeared in what seemed like white goo. I stepped forward and kissed his pink lips, spotting the extra sparkle around his beautiful brown eyes. "You look stunning, Bunny. You smell very sweet too."

He giggled. "I made the frosting for your cake, and the hand mixer flung cream cheese and powdered sugar all over me. But thank you. You look very handsome. Will you come out with me? I'm watching the steaks on the grill. Mom's going to come out and supervise when she's finished with the cowboy."

"Beau introduced himself to me outside. He seems nice." I wasn't sure what else to say. Tyler didn't sound very happy about Beau. "How does she know him?"

"Old friends, pardon the pun. He's fifty-eight. She said they met a long time ago, but they lost touch. He's staying at Foggy Basin Inn, but I doubt he'll sleep there tonight. Anyway, I'm so glad you're here."

I kissed him for a moment before pulling back. "How was your day?"

"We were busy this morning but able to close at two, so not too bad. Thought about you a lot. Can I get you something to drink? Mom explained that red wine doesn't go in the fridge, so I apologize for making you drink that mess last night. We have some lemonade, if you'd like something non-alcoholic right now."

"That would be great. You look extra beautiful today. Love the eyeliner." He'd taken the time to style his hair so that his bangs were off his face in a swoop toward the top of his head. The sunlight caught a shimmer on his cheeks that made him glow, and my jeans tightened immediately. The young man continued to surprise me.

Tyler's cheeks flushed. "Do you like it? I was afraid it might be too much."

I took his hand. "Not at all. You've said you like makeup and painting your nails. I think anything you do that makes you feel good is fantastic. You're beautiful to me any way you present yourself, Bunny. Never forget that. Now, let's check these steaks. I grill a pretty good hunk of beef."

Tyler giggled, and it shot straight to my heart. "You're carrying a pretty good hunk of beef."

He lifted the lid of the charcoal grill, and I picked up the tongs, flipping the steaks and pressing down on them with my index finger to judge their level of doneness. "How does the cowboy like his steak?"

"Rare, please." We both looked up to see Beau coming out of the house sans cowboy hat. He was carrying a tray with metal skewers, some with shrimp and some with vegetables. They looked damn good to me.

"Sure. What do you do, Mr. Fletcher?"

"Mo, right?" I nodded. Why not? "I own a cattle ranch outside Cheyenne, Wyoming. A thousand head of black Angus and Hereford. How about yourself?"

Tyler zeroed in on our conversation as he pretended to sweep off the patio. "I'm a painter—portraits, not houses. It's more a hobby than a profession. I, uh, I'm a travel blogger by trade. I've never been to Wyoming. I might need to check it out." A white lie, but harmless.

Beau grinned. "Say the word, and you and Tyler—I mean, if you ever want to see the sights, let me know. Marlie has my number. You'd be more than welcome to stay at the ranch."

"That might be a few years away." I glanced at Tyler to see a frown. I wondered if there was anything that could be done about Tyler's parole. Was there any way to get it shortened? I had been in Foggy Basin for a year, and it wasn't bad, but Tyler hadn't seen much of the world, and I was dying to show it to him.

"Oh, yeah, I suppose you're right. You have a place nearby?" Beau seemed interested in me more than Tyler, and I wasn't sure why.

"I do. I live up the hill." I pointed to the small mountain looming outside of town that was an object of contention among the residents of Foggy Basin. My granddad called it Foggy Mountain, but many folks in town referred to it as a hill. I really didn't give a damn.

"Did you grow up in Foggy Basin?" I removed two of the steaks because I preferred mine rare as well.

"I, uh, no. I was a stock hauler when I was younger, and my dad ran the family ranch in Wyoming. I hauled our cattle all over the west, depending on which auctions were holding which sales and getting the most attention. That was how I met Marlie. I got lost when I was headed down to Petaluma for the fall cow and calf pair sale. It was early in my hauling days, and we were still using paper maps.

"I stopped at that diner by the highway where the Ford dealer is now. I needed coffee and directions, and I'll be damned if Marlie wasn't in there picking up a fried chicken dinner to go. When I asked for directions from the young woman behind the counter, Marlie came to my rescue because I wasn't sure how that young woman found her way to work the way she hemmed and hawed about how to get where she thought I needed to go. She wasn't anywhere close."

I chuckled because the guy was trying, but I could see Tyler wasn't buying Beau's friendly nature. "And who was that? One of my mother's friends?"

Marlena came out of the house with a saucepan and a brush. "What are we talking about, fellas?" I wasn't touching it with a ten-foot pole.

"Which friend of yours was an idiot at The Highway Diner?" The bite in Tyler's voice was surprising.

"Oh, uh?" Marlena turned toward Beau and cocked her head.

"The redheaded gal who wore her hair in a ponytail and chewed gum all the time?"

Marlena giggled, and it sounded just like Tyler. "Marilyn Keller. I forgot about her. She was a sweet girl, but she wasn't the brightest bulb in the lamp."

"Marilyn Keller? Who is that?" Tyler came to stand next to me, resting his head on my shoulder as I flipped the steaks again before taking them off and putting them on the plate to rest. Marlena handed me the foil, and I covered them.

I turned to Marlena, who stared between Beau and Tyler. I tracked her eyes and did the same, and then it popped. "I'll be a son of a—"

Marlena stepped closer and took the tongs from me. "Not a word, Leslie."

Shit! Now we had a common secret. Hell, I owed her a secret in return.

Chapter Fifteen
Tyler

I stared at my mother. She put the skewers on the grill, and then cornered Mosby next to her. Meanwhile, I was stuck with Beau. Who the fuck was Beau, and why did he keep staring at me without saying a word?

"So, cattle, huh?" My eyes locked with the cowboy, a battle of wills commencing.

"Yeah. You're a barber?"

Was that hard to believe? "Yes. And a damn good one. Are you a good cattle…? What do you call yourself?"

Beau smirked. "I'm a rancher. I took over my family's ranch in Cheyenne about thirty years ago when my father died."

"It's a legacy ranch? Leslie owns a legacy property on the mountain. That seems like a lot of responsibility. Are you there alone?"

"No. I have ranch hands that help move the cattle around. My daughter and her husband live on the property with their daughter. My brother and his wife live at the southern end of the property. We have fifteen thousand acres."

I nodded. "Your daughter and her husband? How about your wife?"

The man glanced at the ground. "She died two years ago. Cancer."

Okay, I couldn't be mean. "I'm sorry. Losing those we love is never easy." I thought of Mosby and the losses he'd suffered. I didn't want to be patronizing to anyone when it came to death.

"True. How about you? You ever lose people you love?"

The man studied me as he waited for the answer. I glanced down at the patio table. "I really only ever had my mother. I didn't have a father, and my grandparents disowned her when she got pregnant. I've only had one person I loved and thought of as a grandparent, Edith Rey, the woman who owned Shear Bliss where Mom's worked since I was a little boy."

Beau didn't need to know about Mr. Harold. That wasn't his business at all.

Beau's face seemed to fall. "I'm really sorry to hear that, Tyler. Your mother is an incredible woman. The two of you deserved much better."

Why the fuck did he care? They dated years ago before I came along, and it didn't work out. Apparently, his wife died, and he came back to do what? Rekindle an old flame? Take advantage of my mother? Not if I had anything to say about it.

"Ty, dear, can you set the table out here? It's such a pleasant evening." I stood and hurried inside to do as Mom asked. I went to the buffet and grabbed a tablecloth she used outside and the matching napkins that were perfectly pressed.

I found one of the many trays Mom had and filled it with dishes, glassware, flatware, and a few candles to put in the middle of the patio table. I came out and set the table as Mom asked. There was a big smile on Mosby's face as I placed everything.

"Looks beautiful, Bunny." His words of encouragement made me feel warm inside.

"Thank you."

I put the four wine glasses on the table before I turned my attention to Beau. "Do you like wine? Mom has beer if you'd rather."

The man seemed to relax. "That would be great."

"Tyler, may I have a beer, too?"

I turned to Mosby, but his smile told me he was sincere. Maybe Beau didn't want to take a chance on what kind of wine we could get in Foggy Basin? Poor Mosby would probably tell him to steer clear of it too. I had no idea what a cattleman would like, but beer seemed safe.

I hurried into the house to get their beers. Mom was busy taking the shrimp and vegetables off the skewers, and next to her on the counter were two frosted mugs, which were new. "You gonna tell me what's going on with Beau?"

Mom was pouring her special steak sauce into a bowl and wouldn't look at me. That was when I realized there was something she wasn't telling me.

"Marlie? You like that?" I watched her every move.

Mom spun around, and I could see the fire in her eyes. "Oh, you're going to criticize my choices? You're seeing a man who we believed to be homeless not two weeks ago. Where do you have the audacity to judge me?"

Tears immediately sprung into my eyes, so I hurried to the bathroom and closed the door. My heart was breaking. I'd always been supportive of my mom, and I thought she'd always be supportive of me. She had been great while I was in prison, but she was going to turn on me now?

This strange man suddenly comes into her life, and I'm not allowed to question his intentions? Bullshit.

I freshened up my face as best I could and opened the door to see Mosby standing there with his fist lifted to knock. "Are you okay, Bunny?" I flung myself into his arms, sobbing and cursing myself for being so weak.

He pushed me back into the bathroom and closed the door. "Aw, sweetheart, it's okay. Let it out. I know it's hard to think of your mother having another man in her life, but I don't think it's as bad as you might believe. Marlena will always stand by you, Bunny. She loves you very much. It's easy to see."

Mosby rubbed my back and whispered sweet things that made me feel cherished. Mom always made me feel loved, but I'd never felt the love and safety Mosby gave me from anyone other than my mother.

Finally, I calmed down and stepped back, seeing the mess I'd made of my face. Mosby lifted his hands and gently raked his thumbs under my eyes to take away the tears. "Good call on the waterproof mascara."

Glancing into his eyes, I saw the crinkles around them. Evidence that he smiled more than he let on. "Thank you for coming to check on me."

"Always. I'll always check on you to be certain you're getting the best life has to offer. I'll always fight by your side. You can depend on me to be there to cheer during the good times and hold you tight during the bad. I want to be in your life as much as you'll let me."

I was slightly astonished by his comments, but then he kissed my forehead, and a warmth enveloped me like nothing I'd ever felt before. I could feel how much Mosby cared about me. I hoped he could feel the same coming from me.

"I want you to be in my life too."

Mosby smiled. "I want to discuss what we want our relationship to be. Can I spend the night tonight? You don't work on Sundays, right?"

"I'd love to have you spend the night. Sometimes I go to the salon to do the books, but I already did them. I'm free tomorrow. Would you like to do something?" I was excited, which took away the sting of Mom throwing me over for her new boyfriend. It was a selfish way to look at it, and I knew it, but I couldn't help myself.

"Yes. I have a surprise for you at your place, and then I'd like us to go hiking tomorrow. How does that sound?"

"Yes please."

There was a soft knock on the bathroom door, so Mosby stuck his head out. "Is Ty okay?"

He turned to me and smiled. "Are you okay?"

I stood a bit taller and opened the door. "I am. I apologize, Mom. I acted like a child, and I'm sorry. I'm just used to having all your attention, and I was caught off guard by Mr. Fletcher. I'll apologize to him."

Mom hugged me and headed back toward the kitchen. Mosby wrapped me in his arms and kissed my forehead. "I'm very proud of you, Bunny. That was a kind thing to do. You're a wonderful boy."

For a reason I couldn't understand, the kiss on my forehead and the praise made me giddy. It filled me with a warm feeling I wanted to experience every day.

I sent Mosby out to the table while I put three candles on the cake Mom and I had made earlier in the day—past, present, and future. I hoped the future was the brightest for him.

Mom walked over with two more beers sans chilled mugs. She put the bottles on the counter and touched my shoulder. "I'm sorry if this took you by surprise, my love. You know you are my world. You always have been, and you always will be. Just because I have another man in my life doesn't mean I don't love you or won't put you first."

I hugged my mother. "I love you too, and I'll get used to Mr. Fletcher, I promise. Thank you for forgiving me for behaving like a spoiled brat. I won't do that again."

Mom's eyes watered, and I giggled. "Oh, now, don't have a meltdown. Your man won't want to see those red eyes."

Reaching up, I opened the cabinet and handed her one of the single-dose eye drops, taking one for myself. After we dropped, I dabbed each of us with a paper towel. Once I was done, we looked red carpet ready—or ready for birthday cake.

Mom grabbed the matches from over the gas range and lit the candles, and I carried out the cake while she grabbed the beers. "Happy birth—"

We sang the damn song and sounded terrible, especially when Beau joined in, but Mosby's smile was brighter than the candles. Once we finished, he closed his eyes, made a wish, and blew out the candles.

"Thank you all for such a special night. I appreciate it."

Mom cut the red velvet cake, and I scooped the vanilla ice cream. Beau was the first to speak up. "Damn, Marlie. This is delicious."

I took a deep breath and smiled. "You're lucky to have my mom in your life. She's a fantastic cook."

Beau turned to Mom, but she gave him a slight shake of her head, so he grinned. "I definitely appreciate that, Tyler. I hope to get to know you better when I come back to Foggy Basin. I need to head back to Cheyenne, but I'm hoping to take your mama with me."

That was a surprise. I turned to Mom seeing she *wasn't* surprised.

I scanned the yard behind her, trying to figure out what to say. "I—. Uh, Edina can manage the salon. I'll rebook your clients if they're not willing to allow someone else to handle their hair needs—how long will you be gone, Mom?"

Mom stared at me with a tender smile. "I'll call Edina, but Ty, I want you to manage the salon. If any of my clients don't want to be serviced by Edina, Camila, Alice, or you, tell them to find another salon."

I was a bit stunned, but I nodded. "Whatever you want, Mom."

She hugged me, and Beau extended his hand. I reached out and shook it. If he made Mom happy, then who was I to object?

"Are you okay, Bunny?"

Was I? Hell, I wasn't sure, but Mom had been happy when I'd shaken Beau's hand, and honestly, if she was happy, I had no right to question it. She'd stuck by me while I was in prison, calling me and coming to visit when she could.

She'd sent me care packages in the beginning, as if I was away at college until I told her to stop because KC took everything she sent. It broke my heart back then, but I appreciated her loving gesture.

"I think so. You're right. I have to learn to share." I sighed heavily as Mosby pulled into the alley behind the salon. He parked next to an odd vehicle. It looked like a small truck with a bed, though it was much smaller than any truck I'd ever seen.

"Who parked that here?"

"An inconsiderate asshole, I'm sure." Mosby stepped out of the Bronco and walked over to the vehicle. I got out to join him.

"What is it?"

Mosby reached into the seat and picked up an envelope with my name on the front. "It appears to be a Polaris ATV. It looks pretty sturdy."

I took the envelope and opened it. Inside was a note.

> *Bunny—*
>
> *I researched this and contacted a lawyer to confirm. I know you can't drive a car right now, and you won't*

> *have a driver's license for a few years, but in this, you can drive around town without a problem.*
>
> *I want you to be able to come to the cabin, and I'm told this will get you there easily.*
>
> *Please don't reject this. It's mine, but I want you to use it. I think we'll have a lot of fun with it.*
>
> *Daddy*

A set of keys fell out of it into my right hand, and I turned to Mosby. "Is this from you?"

Mosby grinned. "What if it is?"

"I don't need a father, okay? I definitely don't need you to be my father." Something about it had me keyed up, but I wasn't sure what.

Mosby stepped forward and took my hands, pulling me over to the ATV. He helped me get behind the wheel and then slid in beside me.

"Bunny, you can drive this around town and up the hill without the police giving you trouble. I've looked at this up and down, and you're well within your rights to drive an ATV up to the cabin without a driver's license. There's a gate on Mountain View Road with a trail straight up to the cabin. Tomorrow, I'll ride up with you so you know the way."

I stared at him in disbelief. Was he for real? Nobody had ever... My mom had tried, but she couldn't give me... What was I supposed to say?

Chapter Sixteen
Mosby

I shoved the keys into the starter and stared at Tyler. "If you don't want it, I'll return it, but I really want you to have it. I love the idea of you driving around town in it. I thought you needed some independence, and I hoped this might give it to you."

Tyler turned his beautiful eyes to me. "Why did you sign the note with *Daddy*?"

It was time to discuss things with him, and I hoped to hell I hadn't read things wrong. The earlier circumstances had made me doubt my idea, but maybe I was still on the right track with Tyler.

"You seem to appreciate it when I offer you advice or suggestions. Have you ever heard of a Daddy/boy relationship?"

Tyler's face froze. "Like I'd wear diapers and suck my thumb?"

It was my turn to laugh. "No. That's age-play, and I don't think either of us is into that. I mean, we could experiment if that interests you, but that wasn't what I meant. Though I'm glad you're familiar with the concept.

"What I hope you'll see is that I want to help you figure out your next steps in life. I want to be your sounding board and safe place to land if things don't work out. I'm not trying to be your father. I want to be your lover, and I want to be your Daddy. You'll always have me on your side as your support system, Bunny."

My beautiful Tyler stared at me, and I was beginning to believe I'd judged everything completely wrong. "If you're not interested—"

Tyler touched my hand. "No, I didn't say that. I'm really trying to figure out what it means."

"Let's take a ride around town. I'll try to explain it to you as we go."

After Tyler started the ignition, I explained how to back the ATV out of the spot and then how to drive forward. "Turn onto Main Street, and let's take a slow ride for you to get used to driving it."

Tyler's giggle had me laughing as we drove through Foggy Basin. He stopped at the two stop signs on Main Street, and when we got to the end of the street, he turned off the motor and turned to me.

"Tell me what you'd expect from me if you were my Daddy."

It was only fair. If he'd never been exposed to a Daddy/boy dynamic, of course, he'd want more information. I wouldn't die if he wasn't interested, but there was a draw to have him look to me for guidance.

"You're beautiful, Bunny. I would never demand things from you. I just want to help you find your way in life and be there to see you succeed."

Tyler stared at me. "Why? I'm a horrible mess, Mosby. Mom tried to offer me advice, but—"

"She's a wonderful woman, Bunny, but there might be some things she doesn't understand about having a beautiful gay son who loved being a butterfly. I see you as a butterfly, sweetheart. I want to support you."

"The makeup? It doesn't bother you? I could tell Mom wasn't too happy about it when I got there, but she didn't say anything. I think it was more because she wanted me to meet Beau than being embarrassed of me. What do you think?"

Damn, I really didn't want to rat Marlena out, and I firmly believed she and Beau should be the ones to tell him the big family secret, but maybe I could help smooth the way. I was unhappy about being put in the position of keeping something from Tyler, but I would give his mother a few days to rectify the situation before I acted.

"Well, I think Beau is from a more conservative area, and she didn't want him to judge you based on your appearance alone. She believes you're incredible, and she wanted Beau to see that as well, but I'd bet she didn't want him to judge you because you enjoy standing out. I'd bet if you went to his place, everyone walking around would be dressed exactly like him."

And thank heaven, that wasn't anything Tyler had to worry about for three years. He definitely couldn't leave the state before his parole expired.

"You've got a point there. My school was like that. Would you punish me if I did something you didn't like?" We were parked under a dusk-to-dawn light, and as I stared into Tyler's eyes, I could see he had a mischievous look.

I chuckled. "Do you want to be punished?" I wanted to tell him he'd been punished enough for a lifetime, but I wouldn't mind leaving my handprint on those sexy globes.

"Well, if I did something Daddy didn't like, I'd accept my punishment like a good boy." It was music to my ears to hear him trying the words and finally giving me a big smile.

"Yes, I can see where that might be something we'll need to discuss. Let's go back to your place. I have something else I want to try out. Drive slow." It was a challenge.

When he pushed the pedal to the floor, I knew it would be a beautiful beginning for the two of us.

What the fuck is bugging me? I reached up to swipe away a fly or a bee or whatever the fuck it was. The giggle made me open my eyes.

"Good morning, Daddy." It rolled right off Tyler's tongue as if he'd been saying it for years.

"Good morning, Bunny." I patted his bare ass, feeling him flinch. "Does that hurt? Was I too hard on you?" The previous night had been fun. I'd sucked Tyler's thick cock while I swatted his ass five times on each cheek with a flat palm. He nearly drowned me when his cum flooded my mouth as he hovered above me and held onto the headboard of the bed.

"No. I'll definitely remember to drive more carefully from now on."

I sat up and kissed the top of his head. He was holding a piece of my hair and had been tickling my nose with it. "Are you looking at my tragic split ends?"

"I wouldn't call them tragic. Just a little neglected. I can take you downstairs and trim them a little. How'd you wear your hair before...? I mean when you were painting pictures?"

I saw a flash of guilt for referring to my past with Alistaire, so I gently rubbed his gorgeous ass as he rested his head on my shoulder.

I wasn't a cuddler, but I found with Tyler, I wanted to be. I wanted to hold him and reassure him that he was loved. I hadn't said the three magical words because I was a little afraid. Anytime I'd told Alistaire I loved him, he would smile and say, "Thanks." It'd been very anticlimactic.

"Let's see. When I was painting and had to meet with clients, I kept it shorter, kind of like yours but it's curlier. I kinda like the length I have now, but maybe it could be cleaned up a bit."

Tyler smiled. "Can I shape your beard too?"

I gave a heavy sigh. The chances that anyone would recognize me in Foggy Basin were slim to none, so I smiled. "Actually, I prefer to be clean-shaven. Can you give me a straight razor shave? I used to go to a salon in West Hollywood where the guy did the closest shave and never nicked me once."

Tyler sat up, a proud smile on his face. "If I nick you once, you can turn me over your knee and spank me harder than you did last night."

I laughed. "I'm afraid you might like that too much based on last night's howls. I need to get a paddle." I held up my right hand to show him the bruise where a couple of blood vessels had ruptured during the previous night's activities.

Tyler took my hand in his and placed soft kisses on the discoloration. I held up my other hand, and he kissed it too. "My turn."

I pulled him over my lap and kissed the outline of my hand on each beautiful cheek. I parted the fleshy mounds and licked his beautiful hole. I wanted to savor every moment leading up to our first time making love. The anticipation was exciting, but I knew the actual encounter would be beautiful.

My tongue circled the opening before slowly breaching with just the tip. His moans were like a song, and my morning wood turned into a steel erection in an instant.

"Okay. Let's get dressed."

I was teasing, but the whiney *"Nooo!"* brought a big grin to my face. "Come on, let's take a shower. I'll make sure we're both satisfied. Where're the lubes your friend brought over?"

Tyler climbed off the bed, his beautiful pink cock jutting in front of him, leading both of us to the bathroom. He opened the medicine cabinet and handed the three bottles to me.

"We can mix these two. It'll do exactly what we want."

I pushed back the shower curtain and turned on the water, adjusting the temperature so we didn't freeze our nuts off or scald our dicks. Once it was acceptable, I placed the two bottles in the caddy hanging from the showerhead and turned to Tyler.

"Hop in. We can save some water."

Once inside, I sat on the bench at the end of the stall and pulled Tyler to sit on my lap. "Scoot closer, please." I opened the bottle of waterproof lube, squirted some in my hand, and repeated the process with the silicone-based lube.

"Mixing these together is exactly what we need."

I pulled him farther up my lap until his balls and cock touched mine. "Put your feet up beside my hips and wrap your arms around my neck."

Tyler nodded and did as I said. I rubbed my hands together and then slid my right hand down both our cocks. Tyler's breath hitched, and I had to agree. The sensation was amazing.

Once I was confident he had a good grip on me, I moved my left hand to his pucker and slid the tip of my middle finger inside him. His eyes went wide, and I grinned. "Kiss me, Bunny."

"*Fuck!*" His breathy gasp as I slid my finger in deeper had my orgasm speeding down the tracks like a runaway train. I had to stop myself or the fun would be over too soon.

I released my own cock and continued to jack his as our tongues tangled in my mouth and then his. I continued to finger fuck him, pushing in until I felt the spongy spot that would push him over the edge.

I pulled back from the kiss and looked into those beautiful brown eyes. "When we get to the cabin, I'm going to sketch you naked. I want pictures of your gorgeous body covering my walls for only me to see. Nobody else gets to see you like this, do you understand, boy?"

"Yes! Yes!" His shouts echoed in the stall.

His cock jerked, but only a dribble of fluid released because of our earlier fun as I continued to finger fuck him until he leaned forward to catch his breath and kissed my neck. I slowly removed my finger and released his spent cock. I pulled him closer and held him, gently rubbing his back as he came down from his orgasmic high.

"Daddy... I've never... My brain is fried." He giggled, and I had to laugh with him.

"It'll get better than that, Bunny. My only demand of you is that if we're going to be together in any way, never ever cheat on me. That is the dealbreaker for me."

I stared into his eyes, hoping he could see how serious I was. He could do damn near anything else he wanted, and I'd forgive him.

But cheating? *Never*.

Chapter Seventeen
Tyler

I thought the top of my head would surely blow off after what Mosby did to me in the shower. I'd been missing a lot, sexually. My encounters with KC hadn't been sexual for me. They'd been a means to an end, and I wished to hell I could wash those images and memories from my brain. Maybe replacing them with things I did with Mosby was a great beginning.

"I can take care of this." I reached down to stroke his hard cock as he rinsed his hair. I'd have to get him some better shampoo. His hair was too beautiful for the crap they sold at the market.

Mosby stepped out of the spray and kissed the tip of my nose. "I'll be fine for now. What time do you open the salon tomorrow?"

"Ten. There should be more than enough time for me to get back here in the morning. I'm excited to spend the night with you at your place." That was putting it mildly. I loved every minute I spent with Mosby. I learned so many things from him. Every day brought new surprises.

"Good. I'll ride with you today and then come back with you in the morning and pick up my truck. Is it okay to leave it behind the salon?"

"Yes, of course. I'll text Mom to let her know. Oh, is it okay if I tell her—never mind." I wanted to tell her his real name was Mosby, but he'd asked me not to tell anyone. I didn't want to damage our newfound trust.

"What, Bunny? What do you want to tell your mother?"

"I was just going to ask if I could tell her that your real name is Mosby Leslie. I wanted to tell her that you're a portrait painter and you do wonderful work."

He grinned at me as he turned off the shower. "I told her yesterday when we were grilling. I didn't want you to have to keep anything from her. I meant to tell you last night, but something else caught my attention." He glanced at my crotch and winked, which filled me with flutters in my belly.

We got out and toweled off before leaving the bathroom and going to the bedroom to dress. "Have you thought about me trimming your hair?" I pulled my sweatshirt over my head.

"Yes. Can you bring your scissors and razor to my place?"

"Sure. Do you want a cup of coffee? I'll turn on the coffeemaker before I run down and grab my things."

Mosby stepped into his jeans. "Yeah, thanks, Bunny."

I started the coffee and then grabbed my keys and rushed down the stairs to the back door of the salon. I opened it and went inside, straight to my station. I opened the drawer and grabbed my leather barber pouch that contained all my tools. As I was folding a cape to take along, there was a knock on the salon's front door.

I turned my head to see a young woman a bit older than me, likely, and a tall young man with full sleeves of tattoos on his arms and a large bird on his neck He was bald and had some sort of ethnic design on the crown of his head.

I walked over to the door and unlocked it, hoping I wouldn't be robbed. "Hi. We're not open, but if you'd like to make an appointment, I can do that for you." I kept my eyes peeled for any wrong moves, but I didn't want to be rude.

They glanced at each other and then back to me, smiling. The young woman extended her hand. "Trixie Carlyle, and this is my partner, Chick Gannon." She reached into her crossbody purse and handed me a business card and driver's license, which I found odd.

I handed back the license after confirming her name matched that on the business card. Under her name, it read *Body Modification Artist*. That was an interesting way to say body piercer. Glancing at Chick, I didn't have to ask what he did.

"Okay. Uh, what can I do for you?" I asked, seeing the multiple piercings on both of their faces. They were creative, but I was wondering about the pain. I'd considered getting my nipples pierced once, but the guy in prison who did it was a sadist, and I worried about getting gangrene and having them fall off.

"We were wondering if you had any space available for us to rent. We've been in the area for a few days and noticed there aren't any tattoo or modification salons, and you have this whole building. We're prepared to pay rent and give you a cut of the profits." Trixie offered a sweet smile, and Chick silently nodded.

Just then, the back door opened. "Bunny, what's taking— Oh, hi."

I turned toward Mosby. "This is Trixie and Chick. They're looking for space to open a tattoo and body modification salon. They're willing to rent the space and give a cut of the profits."

Mosby stuck out his hand. "Leslie. Pleasure to meet you. So, you kids are interested in renting space here?"

"Oh, we'd love to rent space here, but it looks as though you're full up."

I saw them scan the five stations in the salon. The area for a sixth station was where the two shampoo bowls were located, so there wasn't anywhere to expand.

"Oh, there's actually a full floor upstairs that could be remodeled to accommodate two chairs." I turned to Mosby, my eyes growing ten times their normal size.

"That's where I live, *Leslie*." My teeth were clenching at that point. What the hell was he thinking? I didn't want to look for a new apartment.

"I know, Tyler, but let's hear them out. Maybe this could be great. If you also got a nail tech upstairs, with a little remodel, Shear Bliss could be a full-service spa."

"We've been to Miller's Point and that little town...uh." Trixie looked at Chick.

"It's not exactly a town. It's a new resort in a spot called Taylor's Corner. The only thing missing is a salon or spa, but you could probably pick up some clients if you advertised." Chick had a kind smile.

"Let's have a seat and talk for a moment." Mosby took my hand and led me to the sofa. Chick and Trixie followed us.

"Are you always closed on Sundays?" Trixie looked around, and a thought overtook me. Our supplies could be worth a lot of money—if one found the right buyer. Surely, they wouldn't rob us, would they? It would likely serve me right for my shady past.

"Yes, unless we have a special request. Mom and Camila serviced a wedding a few months ago, and we opened the shop on Sunday. Mom said it was gorgeous."

Mosby took my hand and kissed it. "That's something else to consider. Do either of you have credentials in California?"

Trixie reached into her crossbody purse and handed a small plastic bag to Mosby. He opened it and glanced at the papers before handing them to me. Was this what he meant by offering guidance? If so, I was completely on board.

I stared at the two pieces of paper, seeing they appeared official and had their names and license numbers on embossed documents. I decided to hold my questions for Mosby until later.

I continued to listen as Mosby asked them questions. It was easy to see Mosby was deft at getting people to give him the information necessary to figure out what they were trying to get. I held his hand and let him lead the way.

"These look legit. Why did you stop here?" Mosby's beautiful eyes shifted between them, and I knew he had my back immediately.

Trixie sat forward on the couch. "We've been through Foggy Basin a few times, and the place is incredible. We see clients come and go from your shop, and they seem happy. What we hoped was we'd be able to offer additional services. Is this your shop?"

The woman turned her eyes to me. "Oh, uh, no. It's my mother's salon. I work here, but she owns it."

Chick nodded. "Then it's a family business. Is your mother around so we can talk to her?"

"Actually, she's unavailable today, but I will certainly pass along your information, and we'll call you." I stared at the two of them to see if they were unhappy with my answer.

Mosby stood and offered his hand to shake. "Tyler will be in touch. Thanks for coming by."

They said goodbye and left. Mosby turned the lock on the front door before he turned to me. "First, why would you let two strangers into the salon on a Sunday when you're here alone?"

I stood in the waiting area, unable to answer him. Why *had* I answered the fucking door?

Mosby stared at me without blinking. "Do you not realize you could have been robbed or killed? Fuck, Bunny, you were in here *alone*?"

I was suddenly on alert. "I-I thought maybe they were lost or something."

My heart sped up because I knew I'd fucked up, but I couldn't imagine why they would've been standing outside the door unless they needed help.

Mosby looked around for a moment and then took my hand. "Do you have your tools?"

I nodded as I pointed to my station. "Yes, Daddy."

He kissed my forehead. "Let's go." We locked up the salon and got into the Polaris.

I was uneasy because I wasn't sure what Mosby was planning to say or do. I loved him, and I knew I'd made a wrong decision by opening that door. I hoped he'd talk to me so I could judge how upset he was. It took me back to prison and KC.

"I told you not to talk to that asshole." KC was upset and that meant I wasn't going to sleep that night.

"He asked me a question, sir. He's a guard." I knew it was coming, so I went to my knees and braced myself.

"Stupid fucker. Get up." I stood, and KC slapped my face. I landed on my ass, and he stepped over me without looking back.

Panic set in, and I couldn't catch my breath. It wasn't the first time it had happened, but I'd hoped it wouldn't happen around Mosby. It made me helpless, and I never wanted to appear helpless around Mosby. I didn't want him to think he'd made a mistake by being with me.

When we arrived at the cabin, Mosby saw me struggling to breathe. He took my hand and led me into the beautiful entry, putting my tools on the table near the door. I was unable to say anything, still struggling to catch my breath. *How stupid could I fucking be? I am worthless.*

Instead of waiting for Mosby to knock me on my ass, I hit my knees. I'd been there so many times it was second nature. "I'm sorry."

"What the hell? Bunny, no. You don't… Jesus. Baby, no." He picked me up and carried me to the sofa in the living room. "Talk to me. What was that about?"

"I don't want you to hate me."

"Hate you? Are you kid— I could never hate you, Tyler."

"How can you be so sure?"

That was *the* question, wasn't it? What could I do to make sure he wouldn't hate me?

Chapter Eighteen
Mosby

When my Bunny hit his knees, I couldn't breathe. *What the fuck?*

"I'm sorry."

Sorry for what? He'd been perfect. "What the hell? Bunny, no. You don't... Jesus. Baby, no."

I picked him up and took him to the leather sofa in my living room. "Talk to me. What was that about?" His eyes were dead. I couldn't begin to imagine what the hell had happened to flip the switch, but I didn't like it.

I stared at Tyler, and suddenly, he blurted out, "I don't want you to hate me."

What? "Hate you? Are you kid— I could never hate you, Tyler."

"How can you be so sure?"

My eyes settled on him, and I could see the hurt he'd covered up. "I can see you're a beautiful boy, inside and out. I can see you're scared about something, and I want to know why."

"*Why?*" His voice was soft and strained.

I stared at my Bunny. My beautiful Bunny. He was stunning but something was haunting him, and I wouldn't stop asking until I knew what it was.

"Yes, *why*? Why did you go onto your knees? Did I do something that made you think that was what I wanted from you? Please, please, Bunny, tell me what happened."

"It's just a reflex, Mosby."

"A reflex of what?" I studied him for a moment, arching my eyebrow at him.

"A reflex of things expected from me when I didn't do what I was supposed to do. KC had rules. When I didn't follow them, he would hit me in the face."

My heart broke. Hearing what he'd gone through made me sick. "I'll never hit you like that, and if what we did last night is too much, you tell me, and it never happens again."

Tyler turned his beautiful face to me and exhaled. "You made me feel loved, Daddy. It's a big thing to me, and you showed me more love than I've felt from anyone except my mother. It was so amazing."

I kissed his cheeks and grinned. "I'm always here. Let's get you calmed down. In a little while, you can call your mom and explain all of this to her. It might be a great opportunity, or it might not. That's between you and Marlena. I'm here for you, Bunny. Only you."

My beautiful Tyler looked into my eyes. "Thank you, Daddy."

It was the most beautiful thing I'd ever witnessed. We were moving into a wonderful space together, and I welcomed it.

Marlena spent two weeks in Wyoming while Tyler successfully managed the salon, not that there was much more to do than he'd already been doing. He had been keeping the books for the salon since he'd returned to Foggy Basin, so that was covered.

Edina, Camila, and Alice hadn't given Tyler any problems, pitching in to make things as smooth as possible so he could ease into being in charge. His mother's clients even allowed the other stylists to handle their hair needs under the threat that Marlena wouldn't keep them as clients if they didn't cooperate.

While Marlena was gone, I talked Tyler into opening up to his therapist about what happened to him in prison. She'd put him on an anti-anxiety medication that we had to pick up in Hartsville, so after he cleared the trip with the sheriff, I drove him to the pharmacy, and after, we'd gone for sushi, which was something Tyler had never tried.

Tyler was becoming more relaxed driving the Polaris to the cabin, which made me very happy. I'd also started making more frequent runs to town because I wanted to see my boy as much as possible. He'd cut my hair, taking off four inches that left it long enough to pull back when I was painting, but easier to style if I left it down. My tragic split ends were no more, and he'd shaved my beard. My face had never felt softer in my life. Because of my Bunny, I was a brand-new man.

I stopped at the salon before going to the grocery store. Tyler had spent most nights with me, and I had the feeling his worry about opening the second floor to offer more services was because he was unsure where he'd live.

He told me he didn't want to live with Marlena again, but I figured Marlena wasn't long for Foggy Basin—though I wouldn't say a word to Tyler. I didn't want him living at her house either. By my side was exactly where he belonged.

I entered the salon, the small silver bell over the door tinkling to announce my arrival. Marlena was at the front desk on the phone, and she held up her finger, signaling for me to wait. I stepped over to the window to look outside and give her privacy.

I'd parked in the public lot across Main Street, and as I scanned the area, I saw the sheriff's SUV parked in front of my Bronco. I wondered what the hell he was doing, but I heard Marlena end her call, so I turned and walked back to the desk.

"Good morning, Mosby." She stood and walked around the desk, giving me a nice hug.

"Welcome back. How was Wyoming?"

She giggled. "It was great. I wanted to thank you for talking Tyler into taking better advantage of the therapist the parole board requires. He won't tell me anything about his time in Folsom, and I might be naïve about a lot of things, but I know something happened to him in there. He wasn't the same when he came home." Her expression changed from a giddy woman in love to a solemn mother worried about her son.

"I'm happy he's making the most of the therapy. I mean, he's required to do it, so he might as well get something out of it. When are you moving?"

Marlena turned to look over her shoulder to where Tyler was happily chatting with a woman while cutting her little boy's hair. He'd told me he had an appointment with German's nephew that morning before he'd left the cabin. He'd been excited, and I was happy for him.

"Has Ty said something? Does he suspect anything about Beau?"

I wanted to yell at her that she was setting Tyler up for heartbreak by not being honest with him, but I held my tongue. I would be there for him and help him process the new information when she finally told him the truth. I wouldn't let him lose all the progress he'd made with his therapy. He deserved a win.

"No, but you can't keep the secret much longer. Tyler deserves to know the truth and decide how he wants to proceed. How did Beau's daughter treat you?"

Marlena exhaled a heavy breath. "Renee wasn't thrilled to meet me, but by the time I was leaving, we'd had a few conversations, and I believe she's at the tolerant stage as far as I'm concerned. She has a little girl, Amber, who's ten. We got along famously."

"What does Renee think about Tyler?" That was my biggest concern.

"Under the circumstances, I can understand she wasn't happy to hear about him at all, much less the fact he's gay. Thankfully, Beau sat down with her and explained our history before I went to visit. I really need to do the same with Ty. He should know Beau was the one to pay his legal bills. He thinks it was me."

"You let Tyler think you paid the legal bills? You know, don't you, that he feels he owes you that money, Marlena? He doesn't do anything for himself because he wants to pay you back for all the money his lawyer cost."

Her face showed surprise. "What? I never said I wanted to be paid back. I said I mortgaged the house because I had no other way to account for the source of the money. See that's why people shouldn't lie."

"Yeah. That's why *you* shouldn't lie." My voice left no doubt about my feelings on the matter.

"Tonight. Bring him to the house tonight, and I'll make dinner for us. That buggy thing you got him is really cute. He gushes about it. Thank you for treating him so well."

"It's my pleasure. I want to give him everything he's ever wanted. Did Tyler talk to you about the couple who wants to rent the upstairs for a tattoo and piercing salon?"

"He mentioned it, but we didn't discuss it in depth. Did you meet them? Do you think they would be a good fit for this?" She held her hand out toward the rest of the salon.

"I do. Trixie mentioned the new resort at Taylor's Corner, and how they don't have a salon or any facilities for pampering. It might be something to consider." I had no doubt it would be a lucrative endeavor if one had the energy to put into it. I knew my Bunny was the man to make it happen.

"Yeah, I suppose it is." With that, Marlena went to greet a client who'd just come into the salon, and I sat on the sofa to wait for Tyler to have a break.

A man in uniform came into the salon and stood at the front. He was either the sheriff or a deputy. I knew Tyler had gone to check in at the sheriff's office the previous Thursday after we returned from Hartsville, so I hoped the man's impromptu visit wasn't bad news.

Edina walked up to the desk, giving me a wave. "Sheriff West, what can we do for you? Do you have an appointment?"

He grinned. "I do. With Tyler. I'm a little early."

That was a surprise. Tyler hadn't mentioned he was going to cut the sheriff's hair. Maybe they had a better relationship than I'd imagined?

"Ty's finishing up with a small customer. Can I get you some flavored water or a coffee?" Edina motioned toward the couch where I sat.

"What flavors?" He looked very interested.

Edina smiled. "Tyler implemented a flavor of the day. We always have cucumber and lemon—not together. Today's flavor is fresh pineapple."

"That sounds good. I'll have a glass of that, please."

Edina turned to me. "You want something while you wait, Leslie?"

"I'll have the same. Thanks, Edina."

When she walked away, the sheriff shifted his gaze to me. "Leslie? Is that your Bronco in the parking lot? It's registered to Audrey Mosby Leslie. I remember Miss Audrey from when I was a kid. She made the lightest angel food cake and always donated three to the fall festival. She must be your grandmother."

Obviously, I couldn't lie to the man. "Yes, sir. Nana Audrey was well known for her angel food cake."

He smirked. "My mom and dad used to go 'round and 'round over that cake. My father would buy a ticket for the basket raffle, even though my mother would make angel food cake for him all the time. He said they were like lead.

"Anyway, son, do you know people are looking for you? George Willis is convinced you're an axe murderer hiding from the law. Why is there some weird private detective peeking around corners, trying to get a picture of you?"

I couldn't hold the laugh. Natalie was ruthless. "I owe the West Hollywood Gay Men's Chorus a portrait, and I imagine Natalie Wu, my agent, has lined up a hundred more commissions because she's not getting paid if my work doesn't sell."

Sheriff West chuckled. "Ah. You're not an axe murderer then?"

I smirked. "Not yet. I'll get her to call off her dog. While we have a minute, if Tyler wanted to take a trip, say to Montecito, that would be within the parameters of his parole, right?"

"As long as he notifies me he'll be gone and gives me contact information, it should be fine." The sheriff was actually a pretty nice guy. So much for not judging a book by its badge.

"How long could he be gone, Sheriff?"

"Twenty-nine days without needing to notify his parole officer. After that, he'd have to file the relocation paperwork and be approved to move to a new jurisdiction."

I nodded. "Can he leave the state?"

The sheriff stared at me for a moment. "He's not planning to skip, is he? He'd end up back in Folsom to serve out the rest of his sentence if he did. When I talked to him last Thursday, he told me how excited he was to be managing the salon while his mother was in Wyoming."

"He was. I was just wondering if he'd be able to visit extended family before his parole is up. He's not planning to skip. He's making a life here, and I doubt he'd be happy anywhere else."

"Sheriff West, I see you've met my friend, Leslie. If you'd like to have a seat in my chair, I'll be right with you." Tyler was staring at me with worry.

"It's okay, sweetheart. The jig is up. Natalie has a private investigator looking high and low for me. Anyway, Sheriff, it was nice to speak with you. I appreciate the information."

The sheriff and I shook hands before he went to Tyler's station, which had been cleaned up after Tyler's young client left. Edina carried the sheriff's pineapple water over and spoke to him for a minute while I took Tyler's hand to lead him outside.

"Tomorrow, I'll fly back to LA to meet with my agent. She's sicced a private investigator on me, and I want to make it stop. Tonight, we are going to your mother's house for dinner, and then I'll stay at your place, if you don't mind. I'll run home and pack and be back here by five-thirty. That's when you're done, right?"

"So, everyone can know who you are now?" His face lit up, and his smile was megawatt.

"Yes. Everyone can know who I am, Bunny. But most importantly, I want everyone to know I'm yours and you are mine."

Tyler's face flushed as he stood on his toes to kiss me. It was a fit-for-public kiss, but it held the promise of so much more.

"I'll see you later." I watched that cute ass go inside before I crossed the street to my Bronco.

I wasn't looking forward to the trip to SoCal, but I'd put off my life for a year. It was time to emerge from the abyss and start living again.

Chapter Nineteen
Tyler

The day had been long and filled with dread. Mosby was returning to Los Angeles, to his old life, though I was guessing it would be a lot different now. Would this be when I lost him? Would he fall back into the swing of things with his Southern California friends and forget all about me? The ache in my chest at the mere thought was enough to double me over.

I went upstairs to shower and change after I cleaned up the shop. Mom left about three-thirty after her last client for the day. She was going to the store and then home to cook, but I wasn't sure if I'd be able to keep anything down.

I went upstairs to shower and change, and just before I got into the shower, there was a knock on my door. I pulled on a T-shirt and shorts before hurrying to answer. When I opened it, there stood Mosby with a garment bag over his shoulder and a beautiful smile on his face. He looked gorgeous in a pair of dark-wash jeans and a crisp white shirt.

"Come in. I was getting ready to shower. Make yourself at home." I took his hand to pull him inside. He dropped his garment bag and pulled me into his arms, kissing me with the heat of a thousand fires.

I glanced at the clock over my television. We were expected at Mom's in twenty-five minutes, but this kiss... Tongues swirling together. Bodies seeking friction. My dick had a mind of its own and wanted to take Daddy to bed.

Mosby pulled away. "Bunny, if we keep this up, we won't make it to your mother's house on time. Did you talk to her about Chick and Trixie's proposal?"

"I mentioned it, but still, I don't know where I'd live. Their idea probably would complement what we offer at the salon, and now, with the new resort, maybe we could pick up some additional business, especially if we hired a nail tech. I'll talk to her about it tonight. I'll be right back." I hurried to the bathroom and turned on the shower.

Twenty minutes later, I joined Mosby in the kitchenette where he was having a glass of water and reading the news on his phone. "Look at this." He flipped his phone around to show me an art magazine article.

THE MYSTERIOUS DISAPPEARANCE OF ARTIST MOSBY LESLIE IS SOLVED!

"Don't bother reading it. It's a ploy to get me to call Natalie. I'll go see her when I'm there. So, no sparkles today?" He stood and pushed in his chair before he put his palm on my jaw. His thumb caressed my bottom lip.

"You're beautiful either way, Bunny, but I love seeing you sparkle." Those words warmed my heart.

"Next time. Let's go. Mom's a stickler for punctuality. So, you're going to stay at your house in Montecito?" I'd never been to Montecito, but I knew it was near the Pacific Ocean.

"No. It's about a hundred miles from where I need to be in LA. I'll stay in a hotel. I will check on the house while I'm in the area, but I don't plan to stay."

We left the apartment and walked down the stairs. The Bronco and the Polaris were parked behind the salon, and it was a beautiful evening, so we decided to walk. "Tell me about your house. Do you miss it?" I had to tread carefully. His memories of his time with Alistaire were tied up in that house, and I wouldn't demean them.

"I loved the house when we found it. It's a white mission style with a terracotta tile roof. It was built in 1964 for some gay movie studio executive who probably hosted orgies every weekend according to what Alistaire found when he researched it. He was going to write a book series based on the house, but I don't believe it ever got past the idea stage.

"There are seven bedrooms and a large den on the second floor, along with a sundeck and an outdoor fireplace. The kitchen, living room, dining room, family room, and solarium are on the first floor. We have a pool and a pool house where my studio is located, and Alistaire had an office built on the other end of the pool house where he wrote. We also have a nice big backyard."

Mosby chuckled to himself. "Sorry. I say *we*, but it's just me, now, isn't it. Anyway, I don't have beach frontage, but the house is only a few blocks from it. I—"

"You miss your life there, don't you?" I turned to study him as we turned down the street where Mom lived.

Mosby put his right hand on the back of my neck as we walked down the street. "I wouldn't say I miss it. I'm finding there's more to life than the trappings of money or notoriety. I lived a superficial existence before I came here. I don't want to go back to that."

He pulled me closer and kissed my lips, stopping us on the sidewalk in front of my mother's house. For a moment I allowed myself to believe we had a shot together. That we would create a beautiful future for the two of us. I could see us living in the cabin with Mosby painting during the day while I worked at the shop and then hiking or riding around his property before sunset. Long nights of lovemaking and quiet Sundays in bed.

"Hey, you two! Come inside. Dinner's almost ready." Mom's voice was like a bucket of cold water, for sure.

We broke apart. "Later, I promise." Mosby led me to the front porch, and we went inside.

I was surprised to see Beau Fletcher's hat on the sofa table behind the couch. I glanced at Mosby. "Did you know he was coming? I didn't see his big truck."

We walked into the kitchen to find Beau drinking a beer while Mom turned on the burner under a pot of potatoes and water. "Hello, Beau. Didn't see your truck." Mosby grabbed my hand and gave it a gentle squeeze.

"Hey, fellas. I started missing my girl, so I flew in for a couple of days." He stood and extended his hand to each of us to shake. I held my hand back until Mosby pinched my ass and cleared his throat. I stopped behaving like a spoiled brat and shook his hand.

"Nice to see you again, Beau." I then turned to Mom. "What's for dinner?"

"I bought a rotisserie chicken at the market, but I'm making garlic mashed potatoes and have a broccoli salad in the fridge. Everything okay at the salon when you closed? I saw Clay West was letting you cut his hair. How'd that come about?" Mom gave the raw potatoes a fistful of salt and stirred the water just beginning to boil.

"He asked me last Thursday when I checked in." I turned to Beau. "You flew in? Where'd you land? The closest airport is Sacramento, right?"

Mom giggled. "Beau has his own plane. He flew into the municipal airport in Hartsville, and I picked him up."

"Your own plane? That must be handy. Wow, can you fly Mosby to Los Angeles in the morning? He needs to go back to check on his house." Where that boldness came from, I wasn't sure. I had a feeling it was a test I didn't want Beau to pass.

He pulled his cell out and pushed a button, holding up his finger and stepping onto the back patio. "Hi, Perry. I need you to file a light plan."

I turned to Mosby. "Look, a free ride."

"Tyler, why would you do that?" Mom was mad, for sure.

"What?" I tried to look as innocent as possible. When I glanced at Mosby, I could see he wasn't exactly thrilled either.

"It's a free ride. It's nice of him to offer."

Mosby raised an eyebrow. "*Offer?* You're joking, right?"

"It was just a suggestion. I didn't mean anything by it. If he's going to be with my mom, he should get used to doing things for family."

"Tyler—" Now Mom arched her eyebrow.

"He could have said no." It was a weak defense.

Mosby scooted back from the table and patted his lap. My eyes grew huge. I could tell he was pissed. Was he going to spank me in front of my mother?

"Sit, Tyler." Mosby then stared at my mother. "Tell him *now.*"

I sat on Mosby's lap, and he wrapped his arms around me, kissing my cheek before he turned to my mother. She was twisting her fingers nervously, a habit I picked up from her as a kid.

"Tyler, honey, I've told a lie for a long time, and I'm so sorry I did, but I believed it was for the best. I didn't want you to feel bad for me, and I didn't want you to get hurt because of something I did."

"All set. Is eight okay, Mo?" Beau sat down and put his hand on Mom's shoulder.

"That's fine, Beau, but you don't have to take me. I can get a commercial flight." Mosby pinched my ass again. Clearly, I was going to be in trouble later.

"Naw. Why have the damn thing if I can't help out a friend. Anyway, Marlie, honey, go ahead."

Mom swallowed. "Beau is your dad, Tyler."

I damn well hadn't expected to hear that. Then, I stared at the man and wondered what kind of an idiot I was. The man looked just like me—well, an older me.

Beau slid off his glasses. "I met your mother and was bowled over by her. Back then, I was a stock hauler and made it a practice to come to Foggy Basin if I had time at all after I met her. I was thirty-five, and your mother was twenty-two. She was pretty and friendly, and I fell in love with her in a hot minute. I was a bastard, though, because I didn't tell her I was married and had a daughter back in Wyoming.

"When she told me she was pregnant with you, I came clean about my family in Cheyenne, and she told me she never wanted to see me again because she wouldn't be a homewrecker. I opened a bank account and put money there for her for anything the two of you needed." From the corner of my eye, I saw Beau studying me, obviously trying to gauge my reaction to the news.

My stomach flipped. *My father? What the fuck was going on?*

I kept my eyes on my mother, waiting for any clue of how she felt about the matter. My thoughts were too jumbled to make sense, so I sat silently on Mosby's lap and concentrated on the gentle caress of his fingers under my shirt. His touch was the only thing grounding me at that moment.

"Tyler, I thought Beau was out of our lives forever. Our affair was a fluke, really. I'm not the kind of person to go after another person's spouse. I fell in love with Beau before I knew he was married, and even though I knew he was a good man, I couldn't live the life of a mistress. That's why I sent him away and said I never wanted to hear from him again.

"He sent an attorney here with the banking information he'd set up for us. It allowed me to buy the salon and the house." Mom's neck was flushed, which was a sign that she was upset.

"Why'd you lie to me? Why didn't you tell me the truth when I got older?"

The potatoes started boiling over, so Beau got up and quickly turned the burner down. He cleaned up the water before walking behind Mom and putting his hands on her shoulders.

"Tyler, I think she was afraid of what you'd think of her. It wasn't her fault I didn't tell her the truth. I didn't tell my wife, Raelyn, until your mother contacted me about your scrape with the law. I wanted to help you, so I needed to come clean with her because I'd been unfair to all of us for too long.

"Your mother's request was coupled with a demand for me not to show up here. She only asked for my help because she loves you and wanted to keep you out of jail. The money left in the account wasn't enough, so she contacted the lawyer to get a message to me. I'm sorry I wasn't here to love and support both of you."

Mom reached up and placed her left hand over Beau's resting on her shoulder. I was still frozen on Daddy's lap. Man, if I ever needed the ability to disappear, it was then.

"Tyler, honey, I'm sorry. You have always been my priority. I've tried to be mother and father for you. I've tried to give you everything I could, and I didn't want you to hate me. I knew you had a hard time in school, and I didn't want to make things harder at home by telling you about your father." Mom dried her eyes with her fingers.

I glanced at Beau. "What about you? You just threw money at the problem—me being the problem."

Suddenly, I was angrier than I'd ever been. I stood from Mosby's lap and exhaled. "I hope you understand that I need to think about this before I say something I might regret. I'm not hungry, so if you'll excuse me."

I walked through the house and out the front door before I took off running. I didn't stop when I reached my apartment either. I needed time to truly process what I'd been told. It had taken me a few years to understand that I didn't have a father when all the other kids did.

Now I had to accept that everything I thought I knew about my life had been a lie.

Chapter Twenty

Mosby

When the front door slammed, I turned back to Marlena. "Is that what you expected to happen?"

She stood and went down the hallway, and Beau took her seat. "This is all my fault."

I sighed. "Well, honestly, I think there's enough blame to go around. Marlena said your daughter isn't thrilled to learn about Tyler. I guess it's convenient that he can't leave California, huh?"

Beau's head snapped up where he'd been looking at the table. "What do you mean he can't leave the state?"

I chuckled. "He's on parole for two-and-a-half more years. He can travel in California with permission from the sheriff, but he can't leave the state or he goes back to jail."

"Shit. I was hoping to bring him up for a visit after Marlie settles in so Tyler knows she's going to be fine. I want Renee and Mark to meet him. I think Renee would adjust to the idea of having a little brother if she met him."

"Maybe. Anyway, I'm going to go check on Tyler. I'll check in later."

Beau nodded, and I left. I looked up and down the street but I didn't see Tyler anywhere. I jogged the two blocks to the salon and took the stairs two at a time. The apartment door was locked, so I pounded on it. "Bunny! Let me in!"

"He was running toward the park." I glanced down to the street to see the mailman, Mr. Bennett, standing on the sidewalk pointing toward Veterans Park.

"Thank you." I hurried down the stairs and ran in the direction of the park. My huffing and puffing reminded me I needed to get more exercise. It had been too long since I'd worked out.

Finally, I arrived at the park. There was little activity since it was a weeknight. I scanned the area and finally found Tyler sitting on a swing at the playground. I jogged over to him. He was crying hard.

I approached him from behind. "I'm here, Bunny." I walked over and touched his shoulder. He lifted his eyes and flew into my arms. I held him tight, gently rocking us back and forth.

When he seemed steady on his feet, I led Tyler to a picnic table under a shade tree. I sat with him on my lap and held him. "This is a shock, I know, sweetheart."

He nodded and tucked under my chin. We were quiet together for a few minutes. I reached into the back pocket of my jeans and retrieved my handkerchief, holding it up to his nose. "Blow, Bunny."

Tyler glanced up at me and smiled before doing as I asked. "Good boy. Are you ready to talk about this just a little? You don't have to do anything about it right now, but I just want to say one thing, sweetheart. I know this is a shock, but don't make any rash decisions until you've had time to think it through."

That was all I was going to say. I knew Tyler loved Marlena with all his heart, and to shut her out of his life would hurt them both. I didn't have my parents any longer. Now, Tyler had a chance at having two parents. I didn't want him to throw it away because it wasn't presented in a pretty package with a red bow.

After he calmed down, we headed back to his apartment, walking slowly while holding hands. "I have the feeling you already knew about this." Tyler glanced at me, his nose and eyes red.

I damn well wasn't going to lie to him. "I figured it out the other day but believed it was your mother's place to tell you. I'm unsure if Beau came because your mom asked him to or if he really missed her as he said, but I believe she needed his support to tell you about this. I told her earlier today it was time to tell you the truth."

Tyler nodded. "I should have seen it. I look in the fucking mirror every morning. He looks just like me."

Releasing his hand, I wrapped my left arm around his shoulders and kissed the top of his head. "Sometimes, it's hard to see things right in front of us. Don't beat yourself up."

"Thanks, Daddy. Man, a month ago I didn't have a father. Now, I have a dad and a Daddy."

We both laughed. "Please, don't mix us up!"

We walked the rest of the way home in silence, but I was sure we were okay. Once we were climbing the stairs, I put my hands on his hips. "Are you hungry? I can run to the store or make us some eggs." I knew he had a dozen eggs because I'd seen them in the fridge when I got some water while waiting for him to shower.

"Do you think Mom's going to move to Wyoming?"

I wasn't ready to broach that subject, but... "I'd say you won't know until you ask her. Do you wanna go back over?"

Tyler stared at me for a moment and then kissed my cheek. "No, I'll see her tomorrow after you're gone. I'll talk it out with her and, I guess, Beau when he comes back. God, I can't call him Dad."

"But you can call me Daddy, right?"

"Easily. I love having you for a Daddy."

He let us inside and took my hand. "I'll make us some eggs in a little while. I need you, Daddy." More beautiful words had never been spoken.

I followed him to the bed and lifted him, crawling onto his small bed with him in my arms. "What do you need, baby boy?"

I put light kisses all over his face before landing on his soft tantalizing lips. The kiss heated like lighting a long wick on a stick of dynamite. We tugged at each other's clothes and sent them flying across the bedroom. Every piece I peeled off him revealed more of his gorgeous flesh I couldn't get enough of.

I licked over the head of his drooling cock, nearly sending him off the bed sideways over top of me. We both laughed, and he pulled my jeans off, my briefs and socks following until I was as naked as my beautiful boy.

"I want you to make love to me. You'll be gone for who knows how long, Daddy, and I want to feel you inside me. Can we?" He put that plump bottom lip out for me, and I was powerless. He had me wrapped around his pinky, and I knew I was a goner.

"We'll get tested. We can go to that place in Miller's Point when I come back, okay?" I reached into his nightstand and grabbed the condoms—lambskin—and the lube.

"Yes, Daddy. What should I do? Will it hurt?"

I slowed down. "Honey, we've done all but this. I've put three fingers inside you and massaged your prostate when I was blowing you. That's close to what we're going to do, but this will be so much better."

His brown eyes sparkled, turning me on even more. "Get on your knees and climb over me so I can get you ready." I flopped onto my back, deciding that having him on top would be better. He could take it slow, though I hoped not too slow. I was dying to put my dick inside him. I'd been dreaming about it for days.

He picked up the lube and opened the cap, squiring some on my fingers as I took him into my mouth. It was the quickest prep I'd ever done, but tasting his precum drove me nuts.

I popped off him and withdrew three fingers from his ass. "Put this on me." I handed him the condom, which he quickly opened and carefully rolled down my length. I slicked it up and scooted him back on my body until my hard prick was just under his hole.

"Go slow. Don't hurt yourself. Bear down as I push into you. I love you, Bunny."

"I love you too, Daddy." He did exactly as I instructed, and slowly, he sunk down on me until his balls were on my abs.

Tyler slowly raised up as my hands found his hips. The slide of him up my cock was the most beautiful torture I'd ever endured. Seeing his lithe body on top of me had my mind spinning out of control.

"God, baby. You feel so fucking good." I lifted my hips to push into him, seeing his head tilt back as I slid over his prostate. I hammered that fucking thing before I flipped us with him on his back and leaned forward to kiss him.

"Daddy, this... Oh, again."

"You're okay? Can I go harder?"

"Please...please."

That was all I needed to hear. I shifted his legs over my shoulder, and I gave him everything I had. Watching my cock gliding in and out of him was the best sight in the world.

"Are you close?" I moved down to bite his nipples. His full body tensed, and he moaned, which started the fire of my climax burning in my balls.

"I'm so close, Daddy."

I went up on my knees and pulled his ass up my thighs, letting my dick fill him as I stared into his eyes. "Baby boy, spray that sweet cream all over me." I spilled more lube in my palm and jacked him as my cock stayed steel hard inside him.

He moved against my fist, riding my cock. It was amazing. Those brown eyes twinkled, and I knew he was the one for me.

"Daddy!"

When he exploded on me, I exploded inside him. Our eyes locked, and when he grinned, I leaned forward and kissed him. How had I been so fortunate to meet Tyler Rockwell? I owed some deity a donation because I'd never seen him coming.

I woke at six the next morning with my morning wood in Tyler's ass, which I hadn't done on purpose. He was moving against me, which wasn't anything I'd expected.

"Bunny, I gotta get up and shower so I won't smell like sex when Beau gives me a ride to LA. You wanna shower with me?" I hoped he did.

Tyler turned over and stared at me, his beautiful eyes filled with worry. "You're going to come back, right?"

I returned his stare before wrapping my arms around him and pulling him closer. "I will return. I have a key to the cabin in case you want to take a little time away. I want you to think of it as your home, too. In fact, I'd say you should give up this space to Trixie and Chick and let them rent your mother's house if she moves to Cheyenne. Move in with me, Bunny. Live with me. Make a home with me."

My beautiful boy stared at me for a moment before he smiled. "I would love to."

How much better could life get?

Chapter Twenty-One
Tyler

I made Daddy coffee at six in the morning. His smile when I handed him the mug was reassuring. The love we shared filled me with optimism until I remembered that my mother had lied to me for years.

"I'll call you when I get there. I'll be at the Hilton, and I texted you the contact information. If you need me, call me, Bunny. I'm always available for you. I love you, and I'm always there for you."

I exhaled. "Thank you for everything you've done for me, Mosby. I could've never imagined anyone like you coming into my life, and I will always be grateful. I love you, and I'm sure I always will."

His face morphed into concern, but I kept the smile. I was surer than ever that I would never see Mosby again. He was going to Los Angeles, and he'd fall into his old life and forget about a pissant like me.

"Bunny, I'll be back in a few weeks, and I'll call or text you every day to be sure you're okay. Please don't give up on me. We have a great future ahead of us."

I hoped he was right.

Chapter Twenty-Two
Mosby

My eyes popped open, and my head was fucking pounding. The stark white room wasn't one I remembered, and the woman standing to my left with a needle in her hand didn't seem at all friendly.

"Where am I?"

The woman shifted her eyes to me. "You're in East LA Doctor's Hospital. You were in a plane crash, but you walked away with a mild concussion."

I glanced down at my body to see my left arm was in a brace. "How about that? I'm a painter."

The nurse chuckled. "It's a sprain. You'll be fine. Do you paint with your left hand?"

"No. My right. I do like having the use of both hands though. What the hell happened?"

"Mr. Fletcher was misdirected to a runway that was occupied. He ditched the approach and clipped a jet landing at the same time."

"Please tell me he's okay. Tell me nothing happened to him."

The nurse stared at me for a moment. "He's in intensive care."

"Has anyone called his family?"

"His wife and daughter are here. His son's on the way. How about you? Can we call anyone for you? The first responders didn't find a phone to contact anyone for you. You're Mosby Leslie, right? You're the missing artist."

That wasn't what I wanted to discuss. Where was my Bunny?

"Mr. Leslie? We need to ask you a few questions."

I opened my eyes, not seeing Tyler but a woman I didn't know. I reminded me of my fall in front of Shear Bliss, and I smiled. "Ask away, but I have one for you first. Where is Tyler Rockwell?"

"I'm right here, Mosby." I turned toward his voice to see him sitting in the corner of the hospital room.

I exhaled. "How'd you get here?"

"Mom and I drove together. The sheriff gave me permission to leave Foggy Basin to come check on you. You don't have the best luck, do you?" That beautiful smile was all I needed to see.

"The two of you patched up your differences?"

"We're getting there. Beau has broken ribs and he had a collapsed lung, but they got that fixed. They're moving him from intensive care tonight. What the hell happened?" Tyler came to sit on the side of the bed and kissed me, which was everything I needed.

"Beau saved both of your lives by avoiding a collision, or so I was told. I don't remember any of it. Is he okay?"

Tyler smiled. "He's going to be okay because my mother and his daughter won't hear of it any other way. How's your head? This remind you of anything?"

Tyler was sitting on my bed with my hand in his. I wanted to feel it every day. "It reminds me of when I first saw you through the window of Shear Bliss, and I bit the dust. Honestly, that was the best day of my life."

He laughed. "Hold that thought." He went to the door of my room and when he returned, my worst nightmare was with him.

"Mosby. Did you seriously think you could get away from me?" There she was in all her beautiful glory, Natalie Wu, the worst and best agent in Los Angeles.

"I hoped I could." I stared at Tyler. "How did she end up here?"

My sweet Bunny giggled, which was everything I needed to hear. "I think she's magical, but there was a story on the local news about you and Beau crashing at LAX because of a misdirection from the air traffic controller. All I care about is that you're alive, and I'm here to see that you get out of this place." He smirked as he lifted his hand and motioned around the room.

"Is Beau staying in Foggy Basin or is he going back home? What about his daughter?"

Tyler smiled. "Mom wants to get him back to Cheyenne so she can dote on him. I met Rence. She's not ready to call me her brother, but that's okay. I'll worry about that family later. It's my family with you I'm focused on right now. And on that note, I'm leaving you with Natalie. Good luck!"

Yeah, I'd need that for sure.

I stood in my studio at the Montecito house with Natalie next to me. "This is fantastic, Mosby." I stared out my studio windows and watched Tyler float in the pool while music played over the outdoor speakers. It was late May, and we needed to return to Foggy Basin the next day—by commercial aircraft. I'd never fly in a small plane again.

"Good. Give it to them without me present. And give them the check back, Natalie. I know you hate the idea of giving away money, but this is a special situation. I've kept them waiting for more than a year."

She rolled her eyes, which was typical for her. "You've lost your focus, Mosby. I'm afraid I must let you go as a client. I've enjoyed representing you, but there comes a time when we all have to move on. You'll be returning to that crappy little town, right?"

I stared at her for a moment before I smirked. "Yep. I'll be going home. Foggy Basin is where I belong. I'll be enjoying the best of what life has to offer because my happiness is tied up in Shear Bliss."

I laughed at the comment, but it was far too true. I wanted to live the rest of my life in Shear Bliss.

Epilogue
Tyler

Three years later...

"I'm nervous. Should I be nervous? They can't say no, right?" I was rambling because I was in a panic. We were in Sacramento at the courthouse—the scene of my sentencing eight years earlier, and I couldn't believe it was finally over.

"They won't say no, and you'll finally be a free man for the rest of your life. More importantly, we can go on our honeymoon. Now, Bunny, wipe that frown off your face."

Mosby kissed the tip of my nose, and wrapped an arm around my shoulders that made me feel better about the whole thing.

We weren't your typical Daddy/boy couple these days, and never had been. Mosby helped me in ways I could have never imagined, and I did my best to make him happy and proud of me every day. He doted on me and let me make my own decisions, though he was always there with supportive advice. I couldn't have asked for more.

Chatter pulled me from my musings as we turned to look down the hallway. Coming toward us was nothing less than a posse. My mom and dad, hand-in-hand. But then, my extended family appeared behind them—Alice, Edina, Camila, Ramon, and German. Tears immediately sprung into my eyes.

"There they are. You told us the wrong office building, Tyler." My mom gave me that half-mad, half-happy expression that signaled when she was disappointed in me. I had only given her a vague description of where we'd be because I wanted to avoid this very scenario.

Mosby smacked my ass, but he was laughing in my ear. "You should have known Marlena would find you. Mothers have GPS on their children."

I giggled. "You have GPS on my ass."

"Of course I do. You're all mine." Mosby stepped forward and hugged Mom. "You're just in time. We're next." He smiled at my family.

Traitor.

I stepped behind him and took turns greeting everyone. I hadn't wanted an audience when I was having my sentencing day in court, but something inside me was jumping up and down that they were there for me when I was meeting with my parole officer for the last time. It was the nicest thing... I was overwhelmed.

My attorney—Arnie Fister—approached us with a big smile. He'd asked to be here when I got my final walking papers, and I was happy to tell him yes. "Hello everyone. Tyler, are you ready?"

I scanned my friends and family to see supportive smiles all around. Then I looked at my Mosby...my husband. We'd gone to the courthouse after we'd been together for a year and gotten married. Our family was still pissed at us, but we'd done it our way.

Mom had made me a partner in the salon when she'd moved to Cheyenne to live with Beau, and I'd rented the upstairs space to Chick and Trixie for their business and Mom's house for them to live in.

Shear Bliss officially offered tattooing and piercing services. We had a nail tech who worked part-time while finishing her bachelor's in finance, and we got a lot of business from the resort. Things were fantastic in my life for once, and I thanked the universe every day. My life had completely turned around since I'd left Folsom.

Mom returned to Foggy Basin a few times a year, and after my parole was closed, Mosby was planning to take me to Cheyenne to meet Beau's friends. I was nervous about it, but at the same time, I was excited.

A few minutes later, my parole officer, Mr. Lewis, stepped outside his office. "Well, we have a little party going on out here. Tyler, why don't you come inside, and we'll finish this paperwork so you can begin your celebration."

Arnie gave my shoulder a supportive squeeze and I went inside with Mr. Lewis. Arnie had aged a bit since he'd defended me at my original trial, but he was still the nicest attorney I'd ever met—not that I'd met a lot of them.

I held no ill will against the man because I was sentenced for my crime. I'd basically turned myself in, and I'd accepted the guilty plea he'd negotiated. I'd been able to spend the last three years in my hometown with my mother. She'd been reunited with the love of her life, and I'd found mine. That was a happy surprise after my years in prison.

Mr. Lewis closed the door and sat behind his familiar gray desk. I'd had to come to Sacramento to meet with him every quarter, leaving me to meet with Sheriff West the rest of the time, and I was glad not to have to make the drive any longer.

"So, you're here for your last check-in. Is everything going well? How's the salon?" Mr. Lewis wasn't flipping through my file, though it was in front of him on his desk. He was the kind of person who remembered things and cared about those assigned to him. He didn't need to review the error of my ways.

"Salon's doing well. We have a full book and are considering adding a small shop at Taylor's Corner Resort. We're in negotiations with the property manager to rent a smaller space. We'd rotate stylists out there for a few days a week as the business required. I'm looking forward to seeing where it goes."

That was no lie. It had been Mosby's suggestion, and it was a wonderful one. He'd found a business attorney, Raissa Patel, and she was sharp. She was handling all negotiations with the resort's holding company. If everything went well, we'd be opening the salon, Shearer Bliss, at the end of the year.

"Congratulations. You're one of my biggest success stories, Tyler. In my thirty years doing this job, I can say I've never looked forward to anyone's fresh start as much as yours. I'm sorry your conviction can't be expunged from your record, but it doesn't appear to be holding you back."

I smiled at him. "Thank you, Mr. Lewis. You've been helpful to me, and if you're ever in Foggy Basin, drop by. I'll give you a razor shave on the house, and my husband will take you fishing."

He chuckled. "If it was any of my other parolees making the offer, I'd see it as a death threat. Thank you, Tyler. I might take you up on that someday."

Mr. Lewis picked up the stamper and mashed it against the paper on top of my folder. He then closed the folder and picked up another stamper, smashing it against the cover before he turned it to me.

Case closed.

Those were two of the best words I'd ever seen or heard. The best ones were when Mosby had said, "I do."

◻

◻◻

If you liked "Shear Bliss," be sure to check out
the rest of the stories from the Foggy Basin Universe!
https://mybook.to/Foggy_Basin_Series

About Sam E. Kraemer

I grew up in the rural Midwest before moving to the East Coast with a dashing young man who swept me off my feet. We've now settled in the desert Southwest where I write M/M contemporary romance. I also write paranormal M/M romance under "Sam E. Kraemer writing as L.A. Kaye." I'm a firm believer that love is love, regardless of how it presents itself, and I'm proud to be a staunch ally of the LGBTQIA+ community. I have a loving, supportive family, and I feel blessed by the universe and thankful every day for all I have been given. In my heart and soul, I believe I hit the cosmic jackpot.

Cheers!

Also by Sam E. Kraemer/L.A. Kaye

<u>The Lonely Heroes Complete Series</u>

Ranger Hank

Guardian Gabe

CowboyShep

Hacker Lawry

Positive Raleigh

Salesman Mateo
Bachelor Hero
OrphanDuke
NobleBruno
Avenging Kelly
ChefRafe

On The Rocks Complete Series
Whiskey Dreams
Ima-GIN-ation
Absinthe Minded

Weighting... Complete Series
Weightingfor Love
Weightingfor Laughter
Weightingfor a Lifetime

May/December Hearts Collection
A Wise Heart
Heart of Stone
Whatthe H(e)art Wants

A Flaws & All Love Story
Sinners' Redemption
Forgiveness is a Virtue

SwimCoach

Men of Memphis Blues
Kim & Skip
Cash& Cary
Dori & Sonny

Perfect Novellas
Perfect
2Perfect

Power Players
TheSenator

Holiday Books
MyJingle Bell Heart
Georgie's Eggcellent Adventure
The Holiday Gamble
Mabry's Minor Mistake

Other Titles
WhenSparks Fly
UnbreakHim
The Secrets We Whisper To The Bees
ShearBliss

Kiss Me Stupid
Smolder
A Daddy for Christmas 2: Hermie

BOOKS by L.A. Kaye

Dearly and The Departed
Dearly & Deviant Daniel
Dearly & Vain Valentino
Dearly & Notorious Nancy
Dearly & Homeless Horace
Dearly & Threatening Thane
Dearly & Lovesick Lorraine

Dearly and The Departed Spinoffs
The Harbinger'sBall
The Harbinger'sAllure
Scotty& Jay's First Hellish Adventure
Scotty& Jay's Second Hellish Adventure

Other Titles
Halston's Family Gothic - The Prologue
The Mysteries of Marblehead Manor
Mutual Obsessions

Milton Keynes UK
Ingram Content Group UK Ltd.
UKHW030858151124
451262UK00001B/62